I0593997

Devil's Choice

Book 3
Old Balmain House Series

Graham Wilson

Copyright

Devil's Choice

Graham Wilson

Copyright Graham Wilson 2018

BeyondBeyond Books Version

Second Edition

ISBN 9780995431324

Reader Reviews

Reviews of Book

If I could give it six stars I would!!! – it is not often a book will bring actual tears to my eyes but this one did as well as keep me up way past bedtime. If it does not touch you similarly I would be very surprised.

I liked this novel - I thought it was well tied in with the two previous novels in the series and was a fitting conclusion to the series. In a similar fashion as the other two novels I enjoyed the author's exploration of themes in this novel such as rehabilitation, homosexuality and realities of prison life done in an open non-judgemental way leaving the reader to form their own conclusion.

Reviews of Series

Five Stars - I'm so glad I got these books in a set. Each book reached further into the story, always going forward, but also bringing the past as the story unfolded. Well-written characters, and such detail that I felt I was walking alongside them as I read. No imagination is needed to see the people and places in your mind. Vivid descriptions brought the time and place to mind easily. Kindle said it would take more than 9 hours to read it. I did it over two days...I could not put it down! I've always dreamed of visiting Australia, and these books just increased that dream. Well worth reading!!!

Absolutely loved this series - I could not put it down, it held me riveted to each story looking for more. I could vividly imagine each tale and description of the places even though I haven't been there. I would recommend this collection to anyone who wants to read about the settlers in Australia passing through generations and the fast paced tale that goes with all the books in the collection. Well Done Graham Wilson.

Wonderful - I couldn't bear to put them down........wishing there were more in the series. The people were so real it's almost like I've met them.

Five stars – A brilliant read, very interesting.

Five Stars - Another fabulous Australian saga from Graham Wilson
I didn't realise at first this was by the writer of the 5 book Crocodile Dreaming Series. It all makes sense now the way this book rolls along painting out the rich history of 19th Century settlers carving out lives creating history. A huge amount of information to handle. Highly enjoyable read.

CONTENTS

Acknowledgements

Thanks to the many people of Balmain who continue to tell me their stories and share their memories which give the foundation for this book. Also thanks to those who have commented on earlier books in the series and encouraged me to keep writing.

Specific thanks to K J Eyre for a structural review of this book and to Nada Backovic for the new covers for this Second Series Edition.

Author Note

I get a range of reader inquiries on the factual accuracy of this book series. To assist I describe real information on which the story is based in Book 1.

In summary all the books in this series are works of fiction and unless stated as fact the characters are not real people and the events are not real events. When I describe locations I know I try to do so accurately. However there are locations I do not know in detail, such as Long Bay Jail, in which some of this story is set. In this case, while I am familiar with the features of the jail visible from outside, I have no real knowledge of its inside or operations. And even if I did know about how it is today I have set events within it in the 1980s when it was substantially different. So, to get a feel for this institution in this period, I read accounts by those who worked there or were inmates at this time, then used this sense of place to help create my story. It is obviously not an accurate reflection however the intent is to create a general sense of a place not to reproduce specific detail. I hope I have achieved this.

In this story some people have objected to my rehabilitation of a hardened criminal, a character who is both a rapist and a murderer, but in later life shows kindness and compassion. I make no apologies for this. I do not think people can be stereotyped into totally good or totally bad. Even those who have done awful things have potential for goodness and redemption, and they may also gain forgiveness from those they have harmed. If you don't subscribe to this view then that is your choice, but I do.

I have also been criticised by some for the paranormal elements of this story, in particular that it is not possible for a child 50 years dead to communicate with the living and befriend a child of similar age many years later. Again I respect the views of those who don't believe such things. But my life has taught me there are many strange and wonderful things that cannot fit within our simple understanding of our physical world. So I accept the possibility that parts of people or their spirits may continue on. Throughout history many have shared my view. It is not something I know for certain but I believe it could be true.

Synopsis of Little Lost Girl and Lizzie's Tale

Little Lost Girl, the first book in this series, is the story of an old house in Balmain and the successive generations of a family who lived in this locality and house. At the centre of this story, is the story of Sophie, an eight year old girl who, in the early 1900s, went missing one day with a school friend and was never found. Little Lost Girl concludes with a modern day search to determine the fate of this long lost girl. Its story is set within the early settlement of Sydney from the 1840s until the early 1900s and, in particular, in the inner city suburb of Balmain. Real Balmain localities form a major part of the story's background.

Lizzie's Tale, Book 2, moves the story forward to the 1950s and 1960s when another family lives in this same Balmain house. Lizzie has the bedroom where Sophie once lived half a century earlier. This unknown Sophie becomes her childhood friend. However Lizzie's own father dies when she is eight and it is just her and her small brother being raised by their mother. So Lizzie must make the incredibly difficult journey from childhood to adulthood as a poor working class girl who becomes pregnant but is determined not to surrender her child for adoption. Instead she runs away to the remotest part of Australia to build a new life for herself, with her small daughter, Catherine.

It is half a love story, half a suspense story, set in remote parts of Australia and it is particularly the story of a courageous young girl, Lizzie, who triumphs over adversity.

The story ends with Lizzie gaining a measure of retribution for the awful things which were done to her when little more than a child.

Prologue

The room has windows with iron bars, a metal door and four empty chairs facing a metal table.

The door opens. A man walks in, hands shackled together, dressed in prison uniform. He looks middle aged, dark hair with flecks of grey, powerful shoulders and hard features. The softening of age is starting to round his body. A warder follows close behind, baton at the ready. The warder points to the seat. The man sits down, wordless.

The door opens again. A second warder enters, baton also in hand. He moves to stand beside his colleague at the end of the table. A few steps behind comes a slip of a girl. She walks inside and looks around, eyes darting from person to person, face awash with anxiety, taking in the seated man with a searching look. She is small and slender. She first looks like a teenager, but is older, perhaps mid-twenties.

The man looks for an instant as if he recognises her, but this passes. He leers at her; it is a long time since he has seen a pretty girl even if her face is drawn and white. The man speaks, unbidden. "Well, well, look what the fairy godmother had brought me; a luscious crumpet for my pleasure."

The girl recoils as if struck. She steadies herself, takes a chair opposite and sits down. She stares at the man intently, loathing and desperation in her eyes. She wrings her hand together, as if to gather courage. Finally she speaks.

"Please, I need to know if you are my father?"

The man leers again. "Who knows or cares about that. I am happy to father any brats you want me to sire. Is that what you are looking for, a new stud?"

She is silent so he continues. "I have had many sluts in my time; perhaps your mother was one of them. Most could not wait to spread their legs for me. A few needed serious persuasion."

The girl's face struggles for control, expressions of outrage, loathing and fear swirling around. She closes her eyes and puts her hands to her face. It seems she is trying to will her hands to mould control back into her features. At last her face becomes is blank.

She gathers her words. "You are one of three men who raped my mother more than twenty years ago. I am the result of that rape. Now I have my own daughter. I need to find my own father, my daughter's grandfather. He is the only person who has a chance to save her life. I hoped you would help me."

The man looks at her, face inscrutable, appearing to think. At last recognition comes into his eyes. "Yes I see it, the face of little Lizzie, Luscious Lizzie. It is true; she spread her legs for me. She was a good if unwilling piece of crumpet, less of a slut than many."

He pauses. The silence continues. The girl keeps her face blank.

At last he speaks. "I will consider your request. But I have a condition of my own if you want my help. You must all visit, you with your own mother, Lizzie, and with your daughter, only you three. Then I will decide."

Now anguish comes over her face. "My daughter is in hospital, fighting for her life. She cannot be moved. But I will ask my mother to come and bring my daughter's photo. Do you agree?"

A longer silence ensues. "I agree."

The girl stands. "I will ring my mother; ask her to come at once. Time is short."

She walks from the room. The door slams closed.

William

Chapter 1 - Ten Years Alone

William sat alone in his cell in Long Bay Jail, Sydney. It was what he did most hours of every day.

The room was a bare shell of concrete, floor and walls a mottled grey-brown, unpainted surfaces imbued with dirt and other unnamed noxious things. It smelt of stale sweat mixed with a vile smell from a refuse bucket in the corner. A steel bedframe bolted to the floor with a thin mattress and a steel table and bench seat bolted in their place, the room's only furniture. A bare light bulb attached to the roof, high up out of reach, gave sharp edged light.

Twice each day William would do push-ups on the floor and chin-ups on the cell bars, though of late he could feel his motivation flagging. Once each day he had an hour to exercise and walk around a small yard on his own. He was deemed too dangerous to be left alone with other inmates so mostly he was left alone by himself. That suited him just fine. Since he had got rid of Martin and turned Dan into a blathering idiot he preferred his own company. Not that he had ever much liked either of them, truth be told. But he had gone along with them over the years and enjoyed the fruits of their success.

But one day he had woken up, knowing he had lived enough of the slime and lies. So he had decided to give evidence against them. The lawyers had promised a light sentence if he named them, particularly Martin, as the instigators of several rapes. They had suggested he say he had gone along for the ride, which was part true.

But that was not the reason he had turned against them. It was because their bullshit and deception finally got to him. They thought they were having a great time screwing underage school girls, taking advantage of those who were weak and could not complain. And he had gone along with it for a while and enjoyed the element of danger.

But it was really a game for rich boys, those with too much money, those who could buy their way out of trouble. Not much courage there. He had found himself sickened when they had tried to wriggle off the hook on those first three trials and had almost got away with it. It had cost them all, cost them plenty. The company Martin had set up had folded and they were all out of work. But, for Martin, it was only a paper loss. Martin and his family had plenty of money salted away, money the shareholders could not get to.

So other people had taken a haircut for Martin's deeds. Most of them were scum, like Martin, so he did not feel sorry for them. But there were some decent people too, people like his own mother, amongst them. She had worked hard all her life and, thinking this business her son was part of was a good investment, she had bought shares, more than ten thousand dollars' worth, bought in small parcels over a decade, using all her spare cash, marvelling at her son's success.

So, when the company went belly up, she took more than a haircut, she had lost all her nest egg, money saved for a time coming when she was on a pension. It was not much money to a rich person like Martin, but to her it mattered. It would have given her a decent life in retirement; now she could barely afford to eat baked beans.

William said it to Martin, hoping Martin might help his mother out.

Martin laughed, saying, "Times are tough for lots of people, so who cares. Surely you can make it up to her from all the money the business gave you over the good years, if it bothers you enough."

William had blown his money on good living as it came in. So he did not have much of his own to help his mother with, whereas he knew that Martin had millions he could afford to give away.

That was what really pissed him off, that Martin did not give a toss about people like his mother; there were plenty other battlers like her who had done all their cash too. Martin treated it like a school boy joke. He heard Martin laughing about it with Dan later that day. Dan thought it was a great joke. Which just proved what a scummy slime ball Dan was too!

In that callous moment his eyes were opened. He felt disgust towards these people he thought were his mates; it was disgust at them and all they represented, and it was disgust at himself for his part. He had always felt a bit cowardly at the way they preyed upon school girls, not that he minded using force to get what he wanted and they had been sweet young things to fuck. But for him it was more about him being a man who took what he wanted than bravery. Whereas Martin and Dan strutted and gloated as if these actions were somehow courageous.

But until the thing with his mother and the money he had never thought enough about it to act. In a flash, on that day, he realised their whole life together was one sick joke. It shamed him they had come to a place where they could steal from poor people without caring.

So he had named them and they had both got twenty years. Despite the prosecutor's promises to go easy, William got fifteen years.

William had never asked for protection because he knew Martin and Dan were cowards underneath. Although he was not as big and strong as Martin he was a match for Dan. He let it be known that if they came after him he would play dirty, real dirty and, if they hurt him, they would get hurt real bad in return. So Martin took the typical coward's way, getting others to help do the dirty work, no doubt for money or other favours.

One day, Martin, Dan and three other big guys who were in on it, grabbed him. Four had held him. The others, Martin first, had fucked him up the arse like a chook, each taking a turn. They were rough and had hurt. When they finished they promised more was to come, day after day. He guessed they meant to frighten him talking tough. But, instead, that place inside him which hated them from before, when he snitched, got a whole lot bigger.

Afterwards he was madder than he had ever been; he could feel the rage burning a hole inside his guts, *he would get even, no matter what happened to him.* But he had not let on.

He found an old piece of steel rod, the stuff used for concrete reinforcing. It was a foot long and as thick as his index finger, with rough ridges along it. He had spent two days carefully sharpening one end to a point, grinding it against the concrete floor of his cell.

A week later Martin was lording it over him in the shower; having self-importantly told him, William, to wash his back. So he had come up behind him, the steel rod out of sight. He had grabbed Martin around the waist with one arm to stop him running away. With the other hand he had arse fucked him with the steel rod, jammed it in with all his strength. He had felt the tearing and ripping as it went in, loving the feel as it tore its way through Martin's soft flesh.

Martin was bigger and stronger than him. But William held him in a vice grip from behind and, even though Martin squirmed like a stuck pig, he could not get away. While one arm kept his grip tightly around Martin's waist, his other hand had shoved the metal rod backwards, forwards and around, several times, feeling it tear its way through lots of places.

Martin was screaming by then. Within a minute the others pulled William away, leaving Martin lying on the floor, half whimpering, half howling. Then the guards had come and dragged him away and locked him into a cell by himself. He could still hear Martin's screams coming down the corridor as they pulled him along. It had sounded so good and it still made him smile inside.

Two days later Martin was dead, peritonitis they called it. They tried to sew the mess he had made inside Martin back together, but it was futile. Martin died hard and bad. William was glad.

So he had been tried for murder, convicted and sentenced to life in prison.

After that, whenever he saw Dan, he would call out to him, "Your turn next."

Dan was already coming apart at the seams in prison; he was everyone's regular bum boy. Twice, since his murder rap, William had managed to get close enough to Dan to stick him. He used a sharp skewer which he kept hidden away for his own protection, once into Dan's bum and once into his leg.

William had made the weapon out of a fragment of a broken hacksaw blade when he worked in the workshop. Now it lived out of sight, pushed into a hole in his boot sole. It was three inches long and a quarter inch wide. It had razor sharp edges which would cut through if you gave it a twist. One quick stab would barely leave a skin mark but inside would be a mess of damage. By the time people realised what was done it would be hidden again. He had it still. One day he would put it into one of those guys eye's just to see what happened. His mouth watered at the thought.

After that he had only to look at Dan and tell him his eye was next and Dan would become a mass of terrified blubbering jelly. Finally, nearly five years ago, Dan was taken to the looney bin. Last he heard Dan was kept tied to his bed all day in a padded room, crazy, crazy.

With a bit of luck Dan would find a way to top himself one day and that would be that. He must think how he could help him do it, the sooner dead the better.

He never felt a moment of regret over what he had done to those two miserable bastards. But he still felt he had let his mother down even though she disowned him once the rape then murder charges came in, unable to bear the shame of what her son had done.

So he had never seen her or any of his family since he had gone to jail, but he understood that. He knew he could never mend the pain he had caused her, but that only made him madder. Still, in his heart, he was glad he had taken one small step towards setting things to rights, even though it was no help to his mother and never would be.

But it was something towards evening the score and tipping the balance back and for this he was glad. Not to mention that the world was a better place now that that piece of sewer scum was dead.

Chapter 2 - Boredom

At first, after the murder rap, William had lived his life fuelled by rage. It had driven him to keep fit; it had been kept alive by the desire to fix up Dan and the other three blokes who had joined in when they took turns raping him.

So, after Martin was dead, he spent many hours, days and weeks making plans to get at them. His first desire was to injure, incapacitate or kill them, whatever caused pain. But now that they were warned that was easier said than done. Until this chance came he made plans to terrorise them instead, thinking of any ways he could to instil fear and the more unpredictable the better.

Dan had never dobbed on him when he stabbed him, the fear was too powerful. Instead he walked half crippled for months after each time. If William could have got closer maybe he could have put the skewer into Dan or another one's guts or face, but the bum and leg stabs had worked well enough and had been easier to get a shot at.

Since then Dan and the other three blokes had hung together whenever William was around. They all kept themselves at least two body lengths away from him. So he dreamed and schemed endlessly about how to catch them out and get close. If he got within range he really would take out someone's eye or rip a hole in their guts.

But then, as time passed, he had watched as Dan had gone to bits and been taken away to the prison hospital. William knew, deep down, that the others had only been Martin's patsies as well; they did not have it inside them to do real stuff on their own. So his anger slowly slid away, replaced by something much flatter, apathy.

He knew he was in this prison for life and he was determined he would not be broken. He would keep reminding people how dangerous he was every chance he got, that was his main source of pride. But he was starting to find it hard to care.

The days began to drift by in a meaningless maze. Then one day he realised ten years had gone by since he had come inside. That day it was like a red light went off in his brain. *I need to do something more than this before a second ten years goes by.*

Ten years for anger and hatred was fine but he needed the next ten years to be different or he would go crazy too. Perhaps he could try to go back to school and learn something new.

The next week he got permission to visit the jail library and look up courses of study, like TAFE Courses. Some places had lessons they would send to people in jail. He would have liked to do a University Course but he had left school at fifteen and needed his HSC to enrol in one. The TAFE Courses only half interested him, they taught manual skills, things like woodwork and metal work. He needed to learn something that would force him to use his brain.

When he was a little kid he did good at school and people had always told him he was smart. But when he dropped out of school the lessons got left aside. While he could read and write he had fallen out of reading much except girlie magazines, and they were all crap really.

Finally he settled on the idea of doing his Higher School Certificate. This would allow him to enrol for university courses. It was supposed to take two years, but time was one thing he had plenty of and he could not see anything that said he could not try and fit it all into one year. He reckoned he could finish the subjects into one year and he sure as hell intended to give it his best shot.

So he enrolled and began his year of study. Now he read lessons and text books in his cell. Twice a week he was allowed to go to the library for an hour to look up things. He had even almost stopped trying to frighten all the other prisoners. Not that he liked them any better but he figured that his study would be easier if he did not spend almost all his life locked away.

He was not sure what he would study at University but courses like law and medicine appealed to him. He found he had a thirst for knowledge along with the sense that he had wasted the first half of his life. He realised study would only be mental exercise; parole was at best a remote distant possibility in a decade or more. He could not find a place inside himself where there was regret or remorse for what he had done, and he was too proud to pretend something he did not feel. So he would not suck up and become a good behaviour boy, no medals for prisoner of the year.

But still, if he could gain a University Degree doing things of interest, that would be an improvement on the last decade of his life, and it would make the passage of time more enjoyable. His only concern was that he did not want guards or other prisoners to think he had gone soft.

So he needed to maintain an edge of crazed terror to keep others in the jail in line, just enough fear to keep respect alive. There was still a hard angry part buried deep inside which could easily break out in a murderous rage if he was pushed. That part had become so essential to his sense of self that he could not bear to lose it.

He decided that for now he would only exercise it from time to time with random acts of rage, violence and verbal abuse, but he would not really hurt anyone, at least not enough to kill or cripple them. That would keep everyone fully on guard and nervous of him. He grinned at the thought.

So he had a goal, a boredom cure. Within ten years he was determined to be a doctor or lawyer or something such, at least on paper, and doing it would keep the boredom at bay. So now it was time for books and learning.

Chapter 3 - Beginning to Learn

William had nothing else to do except study, he was solitary by nature and even though he had not injured or threatened anyone in months, and had started to moderate his behaviour, he had not been deemed anything but a slightly less extreme version of his previous self. He knew that deep down inside him the violent, uncompromising part of his nature was still there.

The one person who had started to talk to him in a more civil way was the librarian, an elderly man who had retired from regular warder duties but was deemed to be of use in this place. The library he minded was not a large building, only the size of couple cells joined together, but it had a mix of donated books and occasional purchases, including a fairly complete set of school books for those prisoners who had decided they wanted to get a qualification starting with their Higher School Certificate.

William knew of three other prisoners were doing the same as him, but only by name and distant sight, he never spent hours in the library with them, as he was only let in for an hour twice a week when no one else but the librarian warden was there. He was allowed to borrow up to five books at a time, and mostly chose books for his school lessons, but each time would pick out one book about something else.

He discovered in himself an almost morbid fascination about medical things and started to wonder if he might one day do a degree in something related to medicine, perhaps nursing or psychology, as he had become interested in both the processes of mental illness and how to treat people with it. He also found medical and biology subjects, like the study of cells, how the immune system worked and how diseases acted, to be of great fascination. So, almost always, he took out one extra book on a medical subject and, each evening after he had finished his dinner, he would use the time to study the contents of this book, sometimes looking at the detailed pictures but most often reading and trying to understand the words of description and explanation. Gradually he found it beginning to make sense to him, as his brain joined the ideas together. This only increased his desire for more knowledge.

During the day he studied for his Higher School Certificate. He had picked science focused subjects, chemistry, physics and biology, along with the required English and Mathematics. His final elective was Geography to allow him to learn about the places and peoples of the world. He had a particular fascination with the Pacific and with the Melanesian and Polynesian people who lived there. He loved the stories from their history about the way they sailed their canoes across huge expanses and navigated, he read about their customs and the varied speculation about their origins.

He had a vague recollection of his mother telling him once that his great grandfather's, a man who had died long before he was born, was a "kanaka", a Pacific Islander from somewhere out there. He had always felt something of affection for the Pacific islanders he had known, partly for their strength, but also because they lived hard and played hard. He had played a bit of football with some of them as a boy, up until his early teenage years. But that got forgotten once he had got tied up with Martin and Dan. Since then he had always enjoyed watching footy matches with islander players who had come to the Sydney Rugby League competition and made good.

He did not much like blackfellas; there were lots of them around Newcastle when he was growing up. They often hung out in gangs like he had. Sometimes they got into fights with him and his mates, often when they had the numbers; he had got a couple good hidings and given a couple in return. But he looked at the islanders differently and reckoned they were kind of OK.

Now, as well as reading lots of things about diseases and medicine, he also actively searched out any books he could find about the Pacific, the early voyages of discovery, the people of New Guinea, the different islands and groups of people spread out across the Pacific. He had no idea if the great grandfather kanaka was a real story or just something he thought he had remembered, but it gave him an interest and a vague desire, if he ever got out of jail, to go off and work or travel somewhere out there. He always looked east when he had that thought, knowing his cell was less than a mile from where the Pacific Ocean began, alongside the coast in Sydney's east.

Sometimes on stormy days or when a strong wind was blowing from the south east he could hear a distant roar like ocean breakers hitting the cliffs, and at times the tang of ocean, a half brine, half seaweed smell would register in his nostrils, reminding him of the vast, ever present ocean just beyond his vision.

Occasionally he thought about breaking out, getting a little boat from somewhere and heading out that way. But first he wanted to finish his learning, get his HSC and then, hopefully, get a degree in something which seemed useful to him.

He decided that he would park all his thoughts of a break out until at least after that. He was pushing forty now so, with a bit of luck and if he pulled back on the aggression, he would be out of here by the time he was about fifty and still have plenty of time to go off and see these places.

So now he applied himself fully to his learning. Within six months, as the hot weather at the end of the year came round, he had pretty much mastered his HSC subjects. He found the learning was easy, the hardest thing was making himself stop to eat and exercise, when his mind was in the zone. He loved the way his mind could now live in other places through letting his imagination run, though he always kept coming back to absorb and understand one more detail, then yet another detail again.

He thought of his mind as having been like an empty warehouse when he began this learning. At first it only had a few remnants of rubbish scattered around on the floor of an empty building shell. Now he had built shelves and the shelves had spaces for storing boxes of objects from across the world and folders of information about these things. The building still had lots of empty spaces but more and of the storage space was being organised and filled. This mass of new organised information gave him a deep satisfaction.

Then it was time for the exams, sitting in the library under the watchful eye of the librarian with a couple of the other students. He left all his exams feeling good about how it had gone, particularly the Science and Geography ones.

He decided that next year, if he got OK marks, he would enrol in a University Degree. In the meantime he would spend his free time reading about his two new interests, the Pacific Islands and the study of medicine. That way if he got into a course about one of these things he would already have a head start.

One day as he was sitting in his cell he got a call from a warder to go to the library. It was just before Christmas, not that he celebrated Christmas, but he had found in the last week, when a few people had put up some decorations around the prison that it had got him to thinking about his mother and his sister and her children. It made him wonder how they were all getting on, wanting to see the little faces, perhaps no longer little. It was such a clear memory of another life, these children holding his hand and sitting on his lap and calling him Uncle Will. He followed the warder down the corridors to the library, feeling a pang for a life lost.

The librarian greeted him with a huge smile, holding a sheet of paper in his hands. He handed this to Will. It was the results from the exams, a list of subject titles with the results running down the other side of the page. He could see that they were all good.

"Well that's one for the record books," the librarian said. "You have got the best marks of anyone who has ever studied here. They are saying next year you should easily get into University and have a choice of courses. Even the big boss, the prison governor sends his congratulations."

"You are certainly a dark horse, William; some of the other screws are starting to say the study has made you soft in the head, turning you into one of those soft handed faggots.

"But me I say, 'Well done!' I know you have put in the hours to learn what you have. Now you don't want to waste the chance to make a better life for yourself one day. They reckon your science marks were right up there near the top for all of NSW, even above all those students whose rich parents pay them to go to fancy schools.

"Considering you had only yourself and a few books to teach you, that is pretty amazing. Pity you did not do your learning right the first time when you were at school. Maybe, by now, you'd be a University Professor if you had."

William found himself grinning back at this man like he was a kid at school. He could not remember feeling really pleased about something and as good with himself for a very long time. He nodded his head and gave the man a gruff, "Thanks."

Still he thought, *Better watch my step, can't have them saying I am soft or something like that; time to nip that idea in the bud.*

He decided that it was time to scare the blokes who had been with Dan and Martin that night years ago, lest the word get around that he had gone soft with his study. There were still two of them in jail. The third had got out on good behaviour last year. He needed to think of how to do something suitable to hurt them a good bit and scare them even more. He might be enjoying learning new things but he was not yet ready to let all the sleeping dogs lie.

He chewed the ideas over in his mind for a couple days. Then it came to him. With his new-found knowledge he knew something that would give them both the most excruciating gut pains and convulsions, but it was treatable and they would not die. He would slip a dose into their food, he knew he would get a chance to do that with all the coming and going and pushing and shoving in the dining room. And their guard was down now that he had left them alone for a bit.

He just needed to work out the dose carefully to make sure he did not kill them, that way no one would look too hard after the event. Then, a few days later, he would let them and their friends know whom they had to thank. From there the word would soon get around the rest of the place.

That would kill off any idea he was soft and keep everyone on their toes. Much better that way as people would be too busy watching him to cause trouble for him.

He acted three days later, getting into the meal line a few places behind them and bumping into each as they came back past, plates full, to sit down. That allowed him to drop a squirt of his medicine, mixed with some sugar to hide the taste, onto each plate.

Sure enough, later that night, they were both screaming in their cells and emptying their guts all over the place. Both spent three days in hospital with a diagnosis of food poisoning. On their return he said to one of their other faggot mates, "You should ask your mates if they enjoyed the medicine I gave them the other night that knotted up their guts. I enjoyed their screams until they carted them off. Plenty more for them or anyone else who gets smart with me. Perhaps one day I will give them a real big dose and they will leave in a box. It would be good riddance to your bum boy scum mates."

Catherine

Chapter 4- Six Years Earlier : Sydney School

Catherine was sixteen and a half when she first came to Sydney to live. She had lived all the life she could remember between Broome and the desert south of Halls Creek. School was in Broome, but her real life was with her aboriginal friends out in the desert. It was where her Mum and Dad mostly lived.

That small place, not really a town, was a clutch of simple houses and one open sided bigger building, with a tin roof like a shed, but with side screens to keep away the insects. It served as occasional school, occasional store or medical clinic, and regular meeting place.

Apart from that there were about ten houses of various sizes and levels of refinement, some with grass and leaf rooves, some with tin roofs and walls. People lived lives mostly spent outside.

Their house was better than some; it had cement floors, windows and doors and a proper bathroom and toilet. It had a solar panel on the roof that charged a battery and gave power for a couple lights. They also had a gas stove and fridge for cooking and keeping food. It had two bedrooms, one with bunk beds for children and the other with a double bed for her parents. The other space was a living area with a kitchen in the corner, a table and chairs in the middle and three comfy chairs at the other end for sitting and reading. There was one bookshelf where her mother kept her treasured books but that was about it. The walls were decorated with a mix of Aboriginal art and some family and community photos.

Her family also spent a lot of time in Broome and Derby where they had a restaurant and food supply business. But, like her, their first love was the desert, the place where their own love for each other had finally come together. Her mother had started the business in Broome when Catherine was a little girl. Now it was run by those who worked for them and her parents did not need to be around it so much. So, for at least two weeks of every month, they would leave Broome behind and head south to the end of the road, where it became lost in the sand hills at the northern end of the Great Sandy Desert.

There was a variable group of between fifty and a hundred other people living there, some who stayed all the time and others who came and went. All except her family had black skins to her white. But they were her brothers, sisters, aunts, uncles and cousins just as much as her own family were. Even though Catherine was a scrawny kid who was just developing a proper woman's body she could chase and spear a goanna or a kangaroo, or bring down a bird with a throwing stick just as well as any of the others.

But, half way through last year, the year when most kids in Broome left school, what her Mum called her Intermediate Certificate Year, her Mum and Dad had sat her down one day in their house in Broome. It had an ominous feel to it, her Mum and Dad with serious faces sitting opposite.

They pulled out a booklet for a school in Sydney, actually two booklets for two schools, to give her a choice.

She had hoped the choice would be whether to go or not but the choice was only between two schools, which one she would choose.

The first was Presbyterian Ladies College in Croydon where her Mum's best friend in Sydney, Julie, had finished her school. Her Mum had told her before that day that it was a finishing school to help the rich spoilt girls of Sydney learn manners and find husbands. Now she had changed her tune and said it was a really good school. Julie had vouched for it too and was happy to pull a few strings to get Catherine a place as a boarder. So if she went there she would have lots of other girls her own age for company. Julie had written a letter to her, Catherine, which her mother handed her. It was encouraging, telling of all the fun she had there.

The second choice was Balmain High School, where her Mum had gone until her Intermediate Certificate. Her Mum had left then to get a job because the family needed the money. Also her Mum was pregnant very soon after she left school, but that was another story. Her Dad and Julie boasted that her Mum had got the top marks that year, was school dux in her Intermediate Exam. But then, as everyone said, her Mum was super brainy; she could do amazing sums in her head and she knew words that no one else had ever heard of, so it was no surprise that she was so clever at school.

That day, as she sat there, her parents told her that, while school in Broome was fine up to the end of this year, Cathy was too smart to finish there. Instead her final two years would be in a school with lots of other smart kids who would go on to University, so as to stretch her mind and build up her own ability.

That sounded like classic parent gobbledygook. But she realised this argument was futile. Instead she had to decide on the choice she did have, which school to go to. In the end she had decided on Balmain High. It would let her stay with her Grandma, Patsy.

She loved her Grandma; she had this really cute house in Balmain, the place where her and her Mum's own childhood friend, Sophie, had lived, even though Sophie had been dead for years and years before either of them lived there. A part of her felt it was weird-crazy to have a long dead friend. But deep down she knew it was true, Sophie had saved her own and her mother's life that time when they got lost in the desert. The memory was bit faded around the edges now, but at its centre it was just as true and real as ever. So she liked the idea of staying in Sophie and her Mum's old bedroom. She hoped that at times Sophie would still visit her, remembering her as the mind friend of her earliest childhood.

She remembered other visits to this place, a timber weatherboard cottage with an old world feel; bright light from the morning sun to a front bedroom with a view to the street and a scent which wafted in from an old gnarled frangipani tree in the front yard, an attic bedroom with a view of distant harbour and city vistas. But the thing she best remembered was the massive gum tree in the back yard which shaded the house and gave a sheltered place for her and her brother and sister to play and from where a kookaburra called each morning and evening in a raucous voice.

So the choice was made, Balmain High School it was. Her Mum wrote a letter to her Grandma, asking if Cathy could stay with her. When the end of January came round the next year she was booked on the plane which took her to Sydney with an overnight stopover in Darwin. She felt very grown up walking around the streets of Darwin on her own. It was now being rebuilt after a cyclone a few years before, much like the ones they got most wet seasons in Broome.

Her Grandma met her off the plane in Sydney. They went back to her house in a taxi. Now that her Mum's younger brother David was grown up and gone off, working in the mines, her Grandma was living alone. So Cathy knew she was pleased to have her come and stay.

Cathy found she liked living with her Grandma; she was sort of cool about lots of grown up things and was a great cook. She found she could have deep and meaningful conversations with her Grandma she could never have with her Mum and Dad. There was something very open and understanding about Grandma. Hers had been a hard life, but she had lived through it and come out the other side. She was incredibly proud of her daughter who had made good on her own, and she loved Cathy's Dad, Robbie, like a son, even though he was not Cathy's real father. Cathy felt just the same about Robbie, too, even though she could remember a time before he was there. From the moment he had arrived he had become the Dad she had never known. Now he was like a grown up best friend, but who loved her just as much as any other Dad.

When she thought about him, her Mum and her brother and sister still at home, at times she got really homesick. But, after a month in

Sydney, she had new friends at school, and she decided she really liked living in Balmain even though she could barely wait for the end of term holidays when she and her Grandma would fly home for two weeks together with her Mum, Dad, brother and sister, a week in Broome, then a week in the desert with her other family.

Balmain had begun to feel like a new home where she belonged. It had something about it that felt like Broome, a village feel, as well as views of the harbour here that were not so different from seeing the ocean there. Both had a community where people knew each other and were friends who had the time to stop and chat.

A jumble of houses and streets made up Balmain, big wide tree lined streets with grand terraces, little laneways jammed full of workers cottages and all sorts in between. Altogether they gave the place a good vibe. Some of friends lived in grand houses that were clearly worth a lot of money, others lived in small shabby shacks, but all mixed together without caring much about their social status and she felt she could equally be friends of all.

The year flew by and soon it was time to go home for Christmas holidays. This time it was just her on the plane. Her Gran would come across in a fortnight, just in time for Christmas. She knew this might be her last proper holiday at home and was determined to enjoy it. Everyone was telling her how hard she would have to study next year for her Higher School Certificate, so she could get into University and have her choice of courses.

She supposed they were right and she had got good marks in her end of year exams, considering that Broome High School was much easier. But, for now, she would enjoy her holidays and freedom.

The six weeks of holidays was over too soon and she was on a plane back to Sydney. The worst thing about the holidays was that she could see her Broome friends were starting to go their own way, boys meeting girls and getting together, others with jobs so they no longer got holidays when she was there. And many of the things she had done in Sydney did not seem to interest these friends much. So they had less to talk about than before. Still they were longstanding friends and she would never forget them and did not want to say goodbye.

But another part of her was also looking forward to seeing her Sydney friends again, hearing what they had done over their holidays, what had they got for Christmas, who had been dating boys, who had been on trips overseas and things like that. So she was half sad and half happy as she caught the plane back to Sydney.

In the end her final year at school was not such a hard year as everyone told her. She found, as she returned to classes, that she had caught up with the others in her first year in Sydney. So in this second year she only had to keep up, not learn twice as much. Julie was great too; she would come around at least once a fortnight and quiz her on what she had learned. Julie was super smart, just like her Mum, and now a corporate lawyer in a big firm that paid her lots. She still worked on women's rights issues in her free time and was always revving Cathy up to get involved.

Julie had never married. But she now shared a nice house with another woman and, even though it was not talked about much, Cathy had seen them holding hands and understood they were like a married couple, doing lots of things together. When Cathy had free time she would sometimes go and stay for a couple nights with them. There was a good feeling in how they were together, like they really loved each other, just the same way her Mum and Dad did.

She was glad Julie had found someone too. She knew how bad Julie had felt about what had happened to her mother, Lizzie, when the men raped her. It had happened when Lizzie was younger than Cathy was now, and she had got pregnant. That thing had made Julie hate all men for a long time. Even now it seemed there were few men that Julie trusted.

Lizzie was long over it. As she said, without it happening there would have never been her, Cathy, and her Mum would have never met Robbie. So Lizzie would say, "Even though it was bad when it happened and for a while after, I would not change places with anyone, not for all the tea in China," whatever that meant.

Cathy had yet to find a man who really interested her, most of the ones at school seemed like boys who had yet to grow up. Sometimes she wondered what it would be like to do it with a man and sometimes she wondered what it would be like with a girl that way instead of a boy, like Julie did. But she was not very curious about it and, as her Grandma said, there was plenty of time to find out about that yet and first she had to finish school.

So she studied away, but not too hard. One day she woke up in the morning and realised that today was the day of her final exam. As she sat in the exam, writing out the answers, it seemed pretty easy and she finished half an hour early. She waited around outside for her friends to come out, not quite knowing what to do with herself.

Finally they were all gathered, sitting on the brick wall that ran along the street at the edge of the school grounds. No one seemed to have any good idea what to do with the rest of the day, but they needed to do something to celebrate the end of school. Eventually two of the boys turned up with a whole lot of bottles of beer and everyone went and sat in the local park just down the road and took turns having mouthfuls of beer.

She was used to having tastes of her Dad's beer and did not mind the taste. So she found, each time a bottle came her way, she would have a good mouthful. Eventually all the beer was gone.

It was mid-afternoon and they were all hungry. So they wandered up to the main street of the town where they bought hamburgers, taking ages for everyone to be served. By this time about half the kids had gone home, but Cathy was in a happy mood and not ready to go home so soon. So about twenty of them found themselves in a bar in the main street of the town, most sipping beers though a couple of the girls had gin and tonics and a couple had glasses of wine.

It was all good fun, laughing and telling jokes about all the crazy things they had done at school and wondering what the next year would hold. A few already had jobs to go to, but most were hoping their marks would let them go to University next year, a mix of courses and places.

Cathy herself had no idea what she wanted to do, she was only half interested in University, but she had no other good ideas either, so she had filled out the enrolment forms for a range of places to make sure that she got offered something.

As afternoon drifted into evening she found herself talking to the man behind the bar, Mathew. He reminded her of her Dad though he was probably only about thirty to her Dad's forty-five. But he had a slightly weather beaten face and the air of someone who had lived a hard life. He walked with a half shuffle in one leg which again reminded her of her Dad and she found it kind of endearing. He also seemed to like talking to her.

At first she thought he just worked there, but after a while it came out that he was actually the owner. She was surprised the hotel was owned by someone so young. She found herself asking him if there were any jobs for barmaids at the hotel.

To her surprise he said, "Yes, I am looking for a couple extra people coming up to Christmas. It gets really busy in the next six weeks, lots of parties and other celebrations. I was thinking of putting a notice in the window to try and find a couple more people who live nearby to help, not fulltime work, but three or four hours a night on busy nights."

Next thing she knew she was lined up for a trial the next afternoon. Mathew said it was to see if she could manage to pour a beer and a glass of wine without slopping it everywhere. He joked he could give her the trial tonight but she was sure to fail, as she was a bit wobbly on her feet.

Finally it was closing time and everyone started to drift off. As she walked out the door Mathew was there waiting for her and the other five friends that still remained. His car was parked right outside. He suggested that he drive them home. None were too sober. He said he did not want any of them getting mugged or hit by a car in their current drunken state.

They all agreed happily. So Mathew got a list of addresses to do the circuit. Cathy said she lived in Smith Street and he said he lived in Rosser Street himself, the next street from her. So it was agreed, he would drop her last as, by then, he would be almost home.

In the end, it was only Matthew and herself left when they pulled up outside her Grandma's house. When he realised where he was he said, "Well isn't that funny. David and my younger brother were good friends at school and, as they lived in the next street to each other, they were in and out of each other's houses as kids. So a few times I had to come here to collect my brother and got to know David pretty well. I have not seen him since he went off to work, but his Mum, Patsy, is a great cook and a couple times she invited me in to dinner as a kid. She was always very good to me. So do you mind if I come to the door and say hello, trust it's OK, I would not want to embarrass you."

Next thing he was invited in for tea and cake, there was even left over dinner in the oven. Before they knew it they were sitting around the table, drinking cups of tea and sharing a meal and stories. Then the story of the job trial came out.

By now Cathy was starting to feel more sober and self-conscious that she had been too forward and made a pest of herself. Neither Patsy nor Mathew seemed to notice. Both thought it was funny and nice that she may get a job in a pub owned by a friend of David.

Patsy said that David would be home for a week over Christmas and she would make sure he visited the hotel and gave her a report on whether her granddaughter was any good at her job, that way she could let her own daughter Lizzie know. Cathy found herself begin to wish that she had looked for a job with someone unknown to her family, but there was no undoing it now.

As Cathy lay into bed she realised she was feeling woozy. She could not remember feeling this way before and realised that, while she had a few tastes of her father's beer and snuck off with her friends to have a few sips of a shared bottle of beer or wine in the park, she had never sat and drunk the way she had today, hour after hour.

At the time it had felt great, now she was not so sure. The bed had a floating sensation and her head felt full of cotton wool. But she knew today was a significant day in her life, like a birthday but more special. Today she had crossed from one life into another.

As she thought this Mathew's face came into her mind, as if he was somehow important in what came next. But of course he had offered her a job if she could pour a beer without spilling it. The last thing Cathy knew that night before drifting off to sleep in Sophie's room, that's how she named it, was two sets of brown eyes looking at her seriously and talking to her. She could not hear the voices but she realised that one set of eyes belonged to her mother and one to Sophie. They were discussing her and this man Mathew. She had no idea what they were talking about.

Chapter 5 - The New Barmaid

Cathy woke up in the morning with a headache, feeling sick and really thirsty. She went out to the kitchen for a glass of water. Her Grandma was washing up the dishes from last night. She took one look at Cathy, came and put her hand on her forehead, and suggested she go and lie back into bed and she would bring her a cup of tea.

As Patsy put her hand to her forehead, Cathy said, "Grandma, the world is all spinning."

"Don't worry, it will pass in a couple hours," her Gran said, laughing. "Not something you want to do every day. But it was a special occasion after all and the good news about a hangover is it always gets better as the day goes by. I can remember a few nights and next days like that when I first went out with your Grandad. I always tried to hide it from my own Mum and Dad. They did not much approve of your Grandfather and would have been even worse if they knew what we had been up to. But it is part of being young and growing up, even though I realise now one should not do it too often."

Cathy went over and hugged her Grandma. "Part of what I like about you so much is you have been there before and understand," she said.

Patsy replied, "We all make mistakes in our lives. I have made more than most. But life is for living and enjoying not hiding in a corner. Now is your time. Go back to bed now for a couple hours and then you will feel much better."

Suddenly Cathy remembered she had promised to go in for a trial for her job today, the thought of beer now made her want to puke. Now she also remembered her forward way with this man, Mathew, and wanted to cringe; nice girls did not behave that way.

She said, "Oh Grandma, was I really that drunk last night? Now I feel I was really silly, asking that man for a job and him offering me a trial today. The thought of beer makes me want to be sick. Do you think I could just not go, ring up, say I am sick and ask to put it off until another day?"

Her Grandma shook her head. "You could do that but it would be silly. He will know the truth; he has seen plenty of people get drunk and knows you do not make a habit of it. He will have a fair idea you have a hangover today. And a promise is a promise; you said you would go, so you must.

"Anyway it is not until two this afternoon, now is only eight in the morning, by lunch time you will be feeling much better. So that is why it is back to bed.

"I will call you at lunch time, then you can shower and put on fresh clothes, that lovely floral dress you got for your eighteenth birthday would be just right. I will cook you a tasty lunch and after that I promise you will feel much better. If you still have a headache you can take an aspirin but by lunch I think it will be gone."

So Cathy finished her glass of water and went back into bed, thinking she would read for a bit until she felt better. Next thing she knew her Grandma was shaking her, "Time to get up."

She sat up. There was the most delicious smell of cooking and her headache was gone. She was starving. She put on a dressing gown and went off to the kitchen.

"Grandma, that smells so, so good. Can I have some now?"

"But of course, pet. Just give me five minutes." So they sat and ate lunch together, savoury mince on toast. Cathy had second helpings.

"I did not realise that any food could taste so good," she said.

Her Grandma smiled and patted her hand. Then she made a pot of tea and served them each a slice of fruit cake. It tasted amazing, too. "Feeling better now?"

Cathy smiled back, "I feel wonderful, the headache is gone, the food tastes so delicious and I feel like I could walk on air. Is it always like this after one recovers?"

Patsy replied, "One needs to feel bad to notice how wonderful it is to feel well. Life is like that, if everything was always the same one would never notice the difference. But because you felt so sick this morning this afternoon the sun will shine brighter, the flowers will be prettier and life will be better because you can appreciate it all with fresh eyes."

"Grandma, you are so wise. I wonder if I will ever get to be as smart as you," Cathy replied.

"You already are, but no time for talking now, your dress is hanging on a coat hanger in the bathroom. Off to shower and freshen up now."

As she walked out of the house and up the street on a perfect summer afternoon, warm but not hot, with a light breeze ruffling her skirt, Cathy felt like skipping. It was as Grandma had said; sky bluer, light brighter; the day was just perfect.

Then she remembered where she was going, to a job trial with a man who had seen her drunk and wobbling as she walked last night, talking rubbish. She felt like turning straight round, coming home and hiding in the bedroom, it was so embarrassing. However she steadied herself, as her Grandma had said, a promise was a promise. But she no longer felt like dancing, all she felt was terror at seeing this man again after having made such a fool of herself last night.

Now she walked slowly, having to force her feet to take each step forward. At last she was there, outside the front door of the hotel. The clock tower, just across the street, showed five to two; at least she was not late. She stood there, heart pounding, gathering courage to knock.

The door flew open and there he was, Mathew, standing before her. His face took a spit second to register her. Then, as their eyes locked, she felt something pass between them; terror but also more coming from her and there was also something appreciative coming from him.

He looked at her, then looked away and then looked again. She felt the blood rise to her face, flushed with embarrassment. She started to stutter out. "I am so sorry about how I was last night."

He cut her off with a wave of his hand, "Don't worry about that, we all do it. I am just trying to get over the transformation, last night a school girl in her uniform, today a gorgeous young lady stands before me. I can't quite believe the change. I had better watch out to make sure all the men who work here don't get too many ideas when they see you."

Cathy flushed an even brighter red, not knowing what to say.

Now this man regathered himself, as if realising his own manners needed improvement. "I am sorry, I am Mathew Jamison and you are Catherine Renshaw, here for a job trial. I have to go out for half an hour but I have arranged for my senior bar girl, Ella, to show you what the job is and see whether you can master it. Come in and I will introduce you."

Catherine felt a flood of relief that this man would not be watching over her. She doubted her ability to hold a steady hand with his eyes looking on. She would be fine with someone else.

Ella was buxom girl in her twenties, dark hair with pink highlights, a bright smile and a friendly manner. Within a few seconds Mathew was gone and it was just the two of them.

Ella said, "I gather I am to show you the ropes then see how you go. Next hour should be quiet but after three o'clock the early finishing drinkers arrive. Then it gets busy for about four or five hours before slowing down for the last couple hours before we close. How long can you stay for?"

Cathy shrugged, "I can stay as long as you like. It is really up to you and Mathew to say whether I am good enough for the job and when I should go home. But I have nothing else I need to do today so I will stay here until I am either not needed or someone tells me to finish."

Ella grinned and punched her lightly on the shoulder, "That's the way, sounds like the job is yours if you want it, at least for a couple days. You can train a monkey to pour a beer, it is really about whether you can give service with a smile, be polite to drunks who want to paw you but not let them get too forward and keep up with all the orders when it gets really busy. And you still need to find time to tidy up and clear away as you go.

"It will take a day or two until we know that so I reckon you might as well consider yourself signed on for the night and, if after a couple nights, it does not work out Mathew will give you your pay check and that will tell you he does not need you anymore. Otherwise your pay will be made up and waiting for you after lunch on Friday. But if he gives you your pay at the end of a night you know he is not expecting to see you back again."

The next few hours flew by, there was lots to remember, names and costs of drinks, where all the different things were kept, how to keep track of three orders at once while the head on the beers was settling.

But Cathy found herself loving it, the banter of the old men, young blokes giving her the eye and a wink, orders coming from all directions and her keeping track of who was next, getting out around the tables to collect glasses and wipe up the spills. She and Ella worked well together and a couple of times Ella said to her she was so glad Catherine was here today as it would be frantic without her.

Mathew popped in and out a few times, though usually he was only there for a few minutes at a time. He would say a quick hello to his regulars and check how Cathy and Ella were both getting on before he went off again.

At last it began to slow down. Catherine looked up at the clock on the wall and realised it was coming up to nine. She wondered where the last seven hours had gone. Now she became conscious that her feet were tired and her shoulders ached from all the hours of standing and using her arms, it was unaccustomed exercise for someone who mostly sat at a desk.

Ella finished serving a customer and turned to her saying. "Well, I think you have done enough for your first night, hard to believe how busy it got and really lucky for me you were here. I am sure Mathew will keep you on. He has been too busy tonight with paperwork and orders to come and talk, but I will talk to him before I close up. So if you write your phone number down I will ring you tomorrow and work out some shifts.

"I am thinking that, as tomorrow is Wednesday and it is usually quiet, you should have it off. But come Thursday, Friday and Saturday if you are free. Those are busy nights when we need all the help we can get.

"Monday is quiet and tonight, Tuesday, is also usually quiet, though you would not know from tonight. I have Sundays and Mondays off. Mathew tries to do Mondays by himself and then have Tuesdays as his bookwork night, with me doing most of the work and him helping if needed. For the rest of the week we have one or two extras. However, as it is nearly Christmas, he is looking for extra help until after the New Year when it gets quiet again.

"So why don't you head home now. I will ring you tomorrow to work out the details from here."

Catherine had a real skip in her step as she walked home. She was tired but felt incredibly well. She loved this job. And she realised she was starving again too. She hoped her Gran had kept her some dinner. Sure enough a plate of roast lamb and vegetables was waiting for her. As she ate it she chatted with her Gran, bubbling with excitement, telling her all the stories of the night.

After that she settled into a regular routine of Tuesdays, Thursdays, Fridays and Saturdays, and a couple times she came in for

Wednesdays when Christmas parties were booked. Mathew never booked her for Monday night, his own main night. There was awkwardness between them since that first day meeting at the bar doors, both self-conscious in the other's presence.

A week before Christmas David came home from his job working on an iron ore mine out of Port Hedland, on the opposite side of the country and not too far from her home in Broome. Catherine really enjoyed his company. On her nights off he would take her out to the many other places he knew around the town.

On the Sunday before Christmas Patsy invited Mathew around for lunch of roast chicken. David was the centre of attention and regaled them with tales about himself working in the west, mining. He had learned to set explosives to blast away the sides of the mountains, other times he worked with the machinery, dump trucks with tyres three times his height, the huge trains that were miles long and hauled the ore down to the port and all the ships that queued up to load.

David had gone up to see Catherine's Mum, Lizzie, and the family for a week about three months ago. He worked at Mount Newman Mine which was only four hundred miles from Broome, though the road was bad, "corrugations that could swallow a truck," he said. He was full of news of her family, including the antics of Cathy's younger brother and sister. Next day the whole family was coming to Sydney for a holiday, and Cathy had been looking forward to it all year.

Mathew joined in the conversation, but said very little about himself, or his family. Catherine's curiosity got the better of her. When there was a lull in the conversation she turned to Mathew and said. "You must be sick of hearing about our family. What about you and your brother, David's friend? And your own Mum and Dad?"

There was a slightly awkward pause, as if the others knew the answer.

But Mathew turned to her with a smile and said, "Fair question, it must seem odd that I don't talk about them. There is not much to say, really. Three years ago my brother, Pete, was travelling around America, he had just finished school the year before. One day he got in a fight with a couple crazy guys. They beat him up real bad. He died in hospital a week later, he never woke up. Eventually they turned off the machine that was keeping him alive."

Catherine gasped, "That is awful." She did not know what else to say so she put her hand on his arm in a show of sympathy.

Mathew gave her a grateful look and continued, "My Dad died when I was young; he was around the same age as your Grandpa when he died. So, after Pete died, it was just my Mum at home, alone. I was working for an oil company in Kuwait, that's in the Middle East, making good money. So it was time for me to come home.

"But my Mum never really got over the shock and died a year later as well. They said she had a heart attack, but I think it was as much from a broken heart. Of course she loved me too but Pete was the apple of her eye, much the same way that David is for your Mum.

Patsy nodded, "I suppose that is true. Of course each is special in their own way, but some losses are harder to bear!"

Mathew went on, "So now it is just me in Balmain, though I have an uncle, aunt and two cousins who live in Brisbane. After I came home I decided I liked living here in Balmain again, I still have lots of friends here. As I had made good money working in Kuwait I used it to buy the hotel. I am gradually turning it into a business which pays its way.

"It was run down when I bought it. The person who owned it before me had drunk most of the profits away. But it is busy and I have paid down a big part of the debts the last owner ran up, enough for it to start giving me back some money to live on. It needs a new coat of paint and things fixed up. But it is paying its way. I hope, in a year or two, it will be making real money again after each week's expenses are covered.

Cathy felt awkward; the others obviously knew all this. She said, "I'm sorry, I did not know. It must've been hard for you."

Mathew gave her a warm, direct smile. "No, I'm glad you asked. Bad things happen which can't be undone. We must get through them as best we can. It is better to talk about it than not."

Then it was desert and a cup of tea. The conversation moved on to the arrival of Cathy's family tomorrow. Soon after Mathew made his excuses, saying it was a pity but he had yet more paperwork to do on this lovely sunny Sunday and must away.

Christmas and New Year passed in a blur. Catherine was busy with work and family things, nights serving at a packed pub, days at the beach playing with her brother and sister like a teenager again.

On Christmas day Cathy woke to find fantastic presents from her Mum and Dad and the rest of her family and friends. There was make-up from Gran, surprisingly up to date in her taste, a push bike from her Mum and Dad to assist her in getting around, of course the obligatory books from her mother as they had similar reading taste, a modern tasteful work outfit from Julie, and couple small, intriguing packages that she had yet to open. One had a card from Mathew and Ella and the other handwriting from her Mum, she was curious what is was because, as she held it in her hands, it seemed to have a resonance from a distant past.

She opened the one from Mathew and Ella, it was a slim and sleek ladies watch, self winding, with her name engraved on the back, and a card signed by both saying, "We love having you work with us and this is to say thank you from us both."

She showed it to others who admired it with her Dad giving her a wink and saying, "Sounds like someone is an admirer."

She blushed and said, "No just work friends."

She still had the small package from her Mum to open and noticed her Mum looking at her inquiringly, as if to say, 'Come on, Open it!'

So she opened it, feeling an anxious excitement. It was a tiny silver locket, hanging on a fine silver chain. It came to her, a sharp memory of another time and place, and with it the face of little Sophie, childhood mind friend, the person out of another time who had come and rescued her and her Mum in their time of need.

She opened the tiny clasp and gazed at a photo of a small girl of another time. She did not know this girl's story, only that those dark eyes even now connected in some out of space and time way with her, a child unknown, friend of her and her mother who had lived long before either was born.

She looked at her Mum inquiringly and the answer was given, "I feel her help to me is given. Perhaps you or others yet unknown will have need of her friendship. I pass and entrust this to you as a special gift.

Catherine put the locket around her neck, feeling contentment come to her from this intimate connection with a long lost friend.

*

In the New Year the whole family went away for a summer beachside holiday on the far south coast of NSW. Robbie's Mum came up from her home near Melbourne and they had two lovely weekends and the week in between, days at the beach, barbeques and playing cards, walks in the mountains and fishing in the inlet.

At the end of the holiday the whole family drove to Melbourne and spent two days at her second Gran's place in Warburton. Cathy thought this was the most beautiful place she had ever been, a country town in a green valley ringed by towering mountains. Her Gran said that sometimes in winter all the high hills around would be white with snow, now they were covered in thick green forest, with clouds around their edges and mist drifting down into the valley in the early mornings.

Finally the holiday was over. Cathy and her Gran, Patsy, caught the flight back from Melbourne to Sydney.

The house in Balmain felt strangely silent and empty as they came home. They were both a bit sad, missing the noise and laughter of everyone else in the house. She walked over to her Gran and hugged her. "I miss them all," she said, "but still I am glad to be back here with you. Somehow Balmain feels like home now." She looked at her Gran's thin face, tears in both their eyes.

Her Gran said, "I am glad you are happy here. It was very lonely for me when your Mum went away and now that David is gone too I feel so lucky to have you here. I am glad you like it too. Our old Balmain house does have a good feeling doesn't it? I have always liked living here.

"You know what, there is nothing in the house for dinner. Let's go to the pub and see your young man, Matthew," said Gran with a twinkle in her eye! Since you started working there it is like being back to all those years ago when David and Peter were forever together and Mathew would call round in the evening to collect his younger brother who never wanted to go home. Then it felt like they were part of my family. Now that I have caught up with him again it feels the same. I feel like I should have invited him around for Christmas but it got forgotten with everything else happening. So tonight we can give him our best of Christmas and New Year wishes."

It was a quiet night so Mathew came and ate with them. They all swapped stories. He had flown to Brisbane for two days to have Christmas with his cousins, so he would not have been around for an invitation from them in any event. But now he was back and his Sunday calendar was almost permanently free.

Delighted Catherine and Patsy immediately invited him for lunch the following Sunday. It was a lovely meal and the three of them sat and talked after for a couple hours. Finally, in the mid-afternoon, he made his excuses and left. This was the first time Catherine had really felt relaxed in his company and, when he left, she felt she had made a friend. She felt tempted to offer to walk with him as he left but felt it might be thought too forward.

In January work continued as usual, though she did shorter shifts from three to seven each night as there was not enough business to stay on until ten when the pub closed.

One quiet night when it was just her and Ella, they fell to talking about Mathew and what it was that drove him. They knew he was away for a couple days and so would not walk in on their conversation unexpectedly.

Catherine had wondered it there was something between Ella and Mathew. They were clearly close friends, and Ella had her own boyfriend who called around from time to time, but yet is was like there was a secret shared between the two that others did not know. A part of Catherine felt jealous of this special bond they seemed to have, not much but a niggle.

So this night she broached the subject, "You know, you and Mathew, is there something between you, you know, not just friends?" She flushed bright red, it was more than embarrassing and she felt stupid to ask.

But Ella just roared laughing. "God help me if there was. My boyfriend would kill me if there was something to find out. But you don't have to worry on that account. We are the best of mates, I have known him since school days, he was a bit older than me, but I was always one for the wilder boys and he was more steady and serious. But our friendship goes back a way and we trust each other and cover each other's backs. For this job that's what we both need. Actually I think he kinda fancies you though."

Now Catherine blushed even brighter red.

Ella laughed out even louder, then gave a subdued smile. "Don't worry, your secret is safe, seems you fancy him a bit too!"

Chapter 6 - An Uncertain Future

January passed by and then it was February. Catherine had got her exam results just before Christmas and they were good. This meant she should have the choice of various subjects and Universities if she wanted. She was inclined towards Sydney University, only because it was close by, and she should have the marks for any of the courses she had nominated. The trouble was she was unsure if this was what she wanted.

At the end of January she was notified of her acceptance to University and could enrol in her course of choice or a range of other options. Now she had to decide but she really did not know what she wanted to do. She had a couple more weeks until the acceptances had to be confirmed. She found herself procrastinating.

Julie encourage her to enrol for Law, her mother encouraged Science, she herself had a slight preference towards the Arts with a humanities focus and subjects like Anthropology and History, but she knew well that there were very few jobs for people working in that field except to be a school teacher. She really did not want to become a teacher.

She had always thought economics and commerce were beyond boring. But now she was working in the hotel she started to conceive an interest in commerce. After all it was about how to make money. She saw that this business she worked for was a money making machine.

She and Ella had become even closer friends. A couple times, when business was slack, they found themselves engaged in deep conversations about what they would do if they had unlimited money; would they open a business to make yet more money, would they give it to charity, would they go off and travel the world and see and experience everything that was out there, would they buy a hotel as Mathew had?

They could see the way the money flowed through the bar and this seemed to be the most profitable bit. Even though the food seemed to make money there were a lot more expenses with it, the ingredients, the chef, serving and cleaning all the dishes, whereas for the pub most of the costs came from the supply of beer and staff wages. They both formed the view that a pub was a good business to make money from, provided you got regular patrons.

But none of that helped Catherine decide what to do with her life and what course or path to choose. She found herself wishing she could talk to Mathew about her options but, despite her working for him, she saw surprisingly little of him. On the nights she worked it was usually only her and Ella. Mathew at most made an occasional appearance. He had also skipped the last two Sunday dinners. She wished she could have an hour or two to talk to him, one on one, she was sure he would have a much clearer idea than her about what were good future choices.

She half wondered about going and knocking on his door, she knew the street number and had walked past a couple times, but each time her courage had failed her. He also seemed gaunt looking of late, as if he had worries of his own. She did not want to burden him with her minor life decisions. So she procrastinated and the days drifted by.

A couple times she asked her Gran what she thought, but her Gran's advice, though sensible, did not take her very far.

"Do whatever you want to dear, and don't worry if you get it wrong. You can always start one thing and then change to something else a bit later if you realise that you have made a mistake or really want to do something different.

"But you should get a qualification; it is something that gives a girl a choice, apart from getting married and having babies. You are much too smart to just stay at home like that."

So while that was alright it did not really take her anywhere. She supposed, when the final day came, she would elect to study Arts-Law at Sydney University, which was what Julie recommended. Even though the Law did not inspire her the Arts part would be interesting and, at the end, she would have a qualification to earn money doing something other than teaching.

She also tried to talk to her friends from school but none of them had much more idea than her about what they really wanted to do. As none of her close friends had a job they were all a bit bored from sitting around at home and they thought of University as their next adventure of life. All of their parents seemed well enough off so few chose to work to get money. They had been mostly spending their summer at the beach and now were ready to extend their social lives to University. Most of her girlfriends were into boys at this stage, experimenting in going out and dating different boys, some of them going on the pill and trying the sex thing. So that was where conversations went rather than the best courses for their future lives.

Catherine had gone to church, at least since she had been staying with her Gran. Though she was not sure if she quite believed it all, and her Grandmother was no prude, she decided she did not want to try the sex thing right now. What the church said about getting married and loving someone first made a kind of sense to her.

She had seen how happy her Mum was with her Dad; that was what love should be like. Even though her Mum had a baby at fifteen and had worked as a prostitute for a bit, that was hardly of her choosing, it was what she did to survive.

Catherine did not need to do anything like that so she would not rush off to bed with someone just because they wanted her to.

So she continued to work at the pub and delay the decision about her future. Finally, with two days to go, she made up her mind, based on impulse. Her Mum showed how successful one could be when they put their mind to a business. Her Mum had lots of brains but her education had stopped when she was fourteen. But, even so, she had used her own business to make her own way in life, not dependent on others. By the age of twenty one, only two and a half years older than Catherine was now, she had made more money than most people twice her age. So, if it was good enough for her mother to go into business, it would be good enough for her.

She filled out the forms nominating business studies as her first choice, a degree in Commerce but with an Arts component so she could study History and other Arts subjects. She felt relieved once she had made the choice. Now she could get on with the rest of her life. One of the men at work was keen on her; perhaps she would go out with him.

His name was Richard; he was in his mid twenties and good looking, though a bit too cute and full of himself for her liking. But he told funny stories at the pub, which entertained her and the others, even if they were not really very nice, often the humour seemed a bit cruel to her.

He had already invited Catherine out to dinner a couple times and at first she had not answered. But her Gran encouraged her to accept, saying "If you like him just go, at least once. It doesn't have to be any more than that unless you want it to be."

On the first night Richard had walked her home politely and gave her a peck on the cheek at the front door. Catherine liked him well enough and enjoyed his company for the evening but did not want it to go any further. She was relieved he had not tried anything more. The next time he asked she felt good enough about him to go out again.

The second time, after dinner and a couple glasses of wine for each of them, he persuaded her to come with him to another hotel, down near the Victoria Road end of Rozelle where a live band was playing. Richard was drinking much more than her; he had gone onto beers when they came here and downed three in rapid succession, whereas Catherine sipped a tonic water.

Then he wanted to dance with her. Somewhat reluctantly Cathy got up with him. She had never learned to dance in Broome and did not have much idea about the moves. So she moved her body round in time with the music, enjoying the beat which pulsed through her body and mind. The next dance was slow. Now Richard put his hand round her body and pulled her in close. She could feel his hands on her bottom massaging it. It made her feel uncomfortable, then she realised he was trying to kiss her.

She broke away and went to sit down. He came back, looking cross.

She said. "I would like to go home now. I am happy to walk by myself if you want to stay."

He decided he would walk along with her and the fresh air seemed to clear his head as they walked along Darling Street. Then he suggested that they cut through the back streets as it was shorter than walking all the way up to Montague Street, the main street which took her home and the way she would normally follow at this time of night. She had thought she might even call in for a soft drink at the hotel where she worked as it was near the Montague Street corner and it would be good to chat to Ella who would still be at work.

However Richard was determined to take the shortcut. So she went with him, reluctantly. Half way along they came to a small park. He said he wanted to sit down and rest for a little while.

She realised he was quite drunk, he was swaying as he walked, so she stopped to wait for him. He sat into the middle of a park seat, half slumped. He asked her to come and sit next to him while he rested.

Catherine sat down near the end, trying to keep her distance.

Next thing he leaned towards her. He put his arm around her shoulders and pulled her against him. Now he was trying to kiss her again. At the same time he put his hand up under her skirt.

She decided she did not like where this was leading. She pulled away suddenly, standing up and stepping back, sliding under his grip. In a second she was three steps away. He was still groping around as if he did not know where she had gone as she looked back at him.

She realised he was too drunk to follow quickly. So she called out thanks for the meal and skipped away, leaving him sitting there looking half dazed but annoyed. Before he moved she turned the corner and was out of sight. In five minutes she was home, glad she got away so easily.

She knew she would not be accepting any more dinner invitations from Richard; he was not really her type. Her Dad always said that people showed what they were really like when they got drunk. She decided then she did not like Richard very much, drunk or sober.

Chapter 7 - Tremors

One Tuesday night in February Ella rang her and said she was feeling sick and asked her if she could manage the shift alone, with Mathew working on the books in the back room available for backup. Tuesday nights of late had been very quiet and it barely needed them both there. So she said, "Yes, no worries I am sure I can do it by myself."

Mathew was at the bar when she came in and smiled in pleasure at seeing her, saying he was so glad she could cover on her own, it was a big help to him not to have to get someone else in.

She smiled back brightly, feeling pleased to see him alone for a minute. Perhaps, at the end of the night, she would get a chance to seek his advice about what was best for her to study. She had made up her mind on that last day and lodged the form but she still felt uncertain about her choice.

She also wanted to ask him what he thought about her continuing to work, perhaps two nights a week once university started. Her Mum and Dad had offered to support her by paying the expenses while she went through University and she knew they were giving her Gran money to cover her living expenses, as well as a generous allowance to her to cover her clothes, going out and other things she did. However she had more than covered all her expenses from her wages since she had started work and could well afford to skip their allowance.

She could even afford to pay her Gran directly for food and other living expenses though she knew it would be hard to get her to take the money. The few times she had tried her Gran had just given it back saying she should keep her money, she was young and should enjoy life and if she did not need money right now she should just save it as one day she surely would need it. So all her pay went into her bank account, steadily building up, and now there was a good balance.

Catherine liked the idea of being self supporting, after all her mother had managed totally on her own since just after she turned fifteen, three years younger than Catherine was now. So she wanted to ask Mathew whether he thought it was feasible for her to keep doing at least two shifts a week once she started at Uni, knowing she might have to swap her days around once she got her timetable. That way she could largely pay her own living expenses and get her parents to stop their allowance to her.

So she was pleased that tonight she might get the chance to talk to Mathew, one on one, about these things. But tonight Mathew looked really tired and gaunt, like he had a month with almost no sleep, so perhaps it was not be the right night to bother him with her minor worries. Well she would just have to see.

She settled into work and Mathew went off to his office out the back. She worked away steadily and the night passed. About half past nine the last drinkers left and then it was just her tidying up. She was surprised she had not seen Mathew in over three hours; he had called in briefly to check she was OK just after six pm and he looked pretty terrible. He did not look like he had been drinking but it seemed like there was something wrong. She felt worried for him. She wondered if it would be rude or nosy to ask him what was wrong, there must be some problem.

When all the tidying was done it was about five to ten. Mathew still had not appeared, which was unlike him. When Ella was here he usually came down for the last ten or fifteen minutes and gave a hand with the final tidying and counting the money, getting ready to lock up. Now she still had the money in the till. She decided to lock the front doors five minutes early and go and check what Mathew was doing. She could not leave the money unattended and go out the back and she felt worried that he had not come in. Plus no one was likely to come for a last drink five minutes before closing.

She walked out to his office. The door was closed so she knocked. There was no answer. He must still be in there because he could not leave without coming through the bar and she would have seen him.

She knocked again, still no answer. She tried the door. It opened inwards, silently. Now she could hear a faint noise, it almost sounded like crying though that did not make sense. She looked inside. At first she could see nothing. Then she made out a shadow in the corner, on the floor. She realised there was a body lying on the floor.

Suddenly she realised that the shape was Mathew, his body lying stretched out, face down on the floor, pushed into a corner, his legs pulled up towards his body. She felt panic.

The way he was lying was not natural, he would not sleep in that position, it looked too uncomfortable. Please God let him not be dead.

Then she realised a sound was coming from him, something between groans and sobs.

Without thinking more she went over and put her arms around him, feeling his thin broad shoulders shaking underneath her like a leaf. She hugged her body to him and stroked his hair, seeking to give him comfort and reassurance, as if a mother to a baby. She wrapped her body fully round his and lay there with him stroking and crooning to him. "There, there it will be alright, I am here now. I will look after you." She did not know why she chose these words but they seemed right.

He continued to shake like a leaf for a few minutes and then it was as if he started drawing comfort for her. Slowly his sobbing and groaning subsided and then it was just the shaking of his body against hers. She stayed as she was, trying to feed him comfort. Slowly the shaking subsided too. Suddenly he shook himself as if to clear his head. He pushed himself off the floor, half pushing her backwards as he rose. She struggled to maintain her balance and not fall to the side as her feet were not fully under her.

He turned his face towards her with puzzlement, as is trying to understand what was happening. He saw her wobbling to hold her balance and reached out to steady her, a firm arm grasping her elbow. "My God, Catherine, what are you doing here?" His eyes flashed; something between confusion, embarrassment and anger that someone had seen him in this state.

She looked back steadily, determined not to be cowed. She said, "It's OK Mathew, when I came in you were lying half curled up in the corner shaking and moaning as if having an awful dream.. Tell me what's wrong? I want to help."

He looked at her, uncertain, as if trying to decide what to do or say.

Catherine tried for a smile, it worked.

She could see some of the tension leave his face as he relaxed, then he smiled back. There was a lounge to one side of his office, a three seater that someone could stretch out on for a sleep. He walked over to it, his body trembling slightly, and sat down. She could see he was making an effort to keep the trembling in check.

She followed him, unbidden, and sat next to him. There was effort on his face now and the trembling was increasing, as if whatever devil was there was returning. Without asking she put her arms around him again and pulled his face against her breast, stroking his hair. The trembling grew worse and worse until his whole body was shaking.

She just held him and kept whispering words of comfort, waiting for it to pass. It went on and on, but after what seemed like a long time she could feel it ease. She sensed she could let him go now, that he was back under control, but she was determined not to. It was as if a primordial instinct told her that the best way to comfort him was with touch; stroking and holding, the way a mother would with a child. In a way she could not explain his needing her and her giving him comfort was the most satisfying and fulfilling thing she had ever done, it felt so right.

Finally, when his body was almost still, she heard him whisper, head still against her chest. "Thank you, thank you, I have not been held like that for such a long time. You have no idea just how good it felt, just to be held and safe."

She whispered back, "Since the day I met you I have wanted to hold you like this, to feel your breath against my cheek. I am glad I've been able to give you comfort and I would give you more if I knew how. Please tell me what I can do to help you?"

It seemed to her as if those words broke the spell of togetherness enough for him to sit up. Slowly he straightened his body until he was sitting straight beside her. He took her hand in his and held it to his face. She felt the roughened stubble and felt a huge desire to caress his face. She rested her hand where he held it and then brought her other hand to his face on the opposite side, running it through his hair then caressing his cheek. With his free hand he reached behind her neck and brought her face to his until their noses were almost touching. Then, light as down, he kissed her on her lips. Her lips sought his out and she kissed him back. Now their mouths were joined in an incredibly tender kiss.

Finally he pulled back, looked at her, eyes bright as if with tears. He pulled her face onto his chest. He wrapped his arms around her and she wrapped hers around him and for a long time they sat there in wordless embrace, each drawing comfort from the other touching body.

She did not know how long had passed, minutes, hours, an unknown quantity. Finally she straightened, knowing the next step was hers to take.

She said, "I choose to stay with you tonight, to sleep with your body holding mine. But first I would have you tell me, what is this thing which troubles you so? It is something I need to know this if am to share your life, as if I were your wife."

He looked at her, incredulous. "What are you saying?"

She replied; it was so simple in her mind. "I think we should be together, even married; that is if you want me."

He said, "Of course I want you, I wanted you since the day you came into my bar and asked for a job, the forward, tipsy, but oh so beautiful girl in the school dress. When you came back the next day in that floral dress, I thought you were the loveliest sight I had ever seen.

"But I cannot understand why you would want me. Me, a broken down wreck of a man; a man of tortured dreams and flashbacks which haunt my days and destroy my nights. Why would you, a fresh and lovely rose of eighteen, want me, a worn out man who is almost twice your age?

She put a finger to his lips, then lay her head back against his chest. "I don't know what it is that makes me want you, to be near you, to touch you like this. But it is what I want, it is right for me and it is right for you. We make each other happy and strong. That is much more than good."

Catherine stayed with him that night. They lay together on the couch, just holding each other and talking, sometimes sleeping, then waking and talking some more.

Matthew told her the story of his life, his going to Vietnam and the horrors there, now the flashbacks and the nights when he relived it endlessly. He also told her of how the Americans had sprayed the forest to kill the leaves and how he had got sprayed too several times, his clothing drenched with foul smelling chemicals, and how, after a few times, he got really sick, lying in bed and shaking for more than a week before he could walk again. They now said that some batches of these chemicals were contaminated with a thing called dioxin which was much worse than the Agent Orange which killed the leaves. He did not know if it was the effect of the chemicals or just all the horrors he had seen, little kids blown apart, women with pregnant bellies lying dead in the water, whole families huddled together in their huts killed when the shells struck, and his own best mate suddenly dead when a sniper's bullet ripped into him.

Most especially he told her of a small Vietnamese girl, an orphan who had become his friend, an itinerant in their camp, how several times she had saved his life and those of his friends by giving him information that protected them. Then one day they had found her awfully mutilated body tied to the camp perimeter. It was clear they had tortured her in an awful way before she had died, they must have found she was an informer who helped him. Now her face and small mutilated body visited him in sleep and dreams along with the other horrors. Until recently he thought it was going away. But this year it had come back ever more strongly, and now it was like he was haunted by a recurring nightmare whenever he closed his eyes.

He had been only twenty when he went to war and he was only there for three years before he was discharged as medically unfit, he had taken a piece of shrapnel in the hip, which gave him a limp. But really it was the shakes which finished him. They would come over him at times and no one could tell him the cause.

So he had come back to Sydney after his medical discharge and the army helped him to get an engineering degree and then a job in the Middle East and where he made really good money. He lived in an oil camp where his life was easy, all meals provided, just work he could do and which kept him occupied and that helped.

He had learned how to mostly live with the terrors and the shakes, though sometimes he had to stay in bed for a couple days until they passed. But he had thought he was getting better and, when he had come home to his mother, he had known he did not want to go back to a solitary life in an oil camp. While his mother lived it helped and things were better, though it had been terrible when she died and he was on his own again.

But after she had died he had pulled himself together and bought the hotel. As well as the money from his former work his mother had given him a modest inheritance and a house. So the house was security and the inheritance and other money paid the deposit for the hotel and the bank lent the rest, though he had to agree to take on the debts owed to various businesses around the area. He would not have wanted it any other way as most of them were people he knew who had advanced services and supplies in good faith, but it added to the burden of the loan.

He was gradually paying back the bank and the other businesses though it took half his takings, and the rest went to pay staff and buy the food and beer. But all had been going well except since Christmas when the shakes and terrors had returned in a big way. Now he was barely able to work and keep the books. So it was all going backwards which was another worry; the money was now getting wobbly again. Ella sort of knew and covered for him, not all the details, but a couple times she had found him shaking and had put an arm around his shoulders and made him a cup of tea, and that had helped. But it had never been as bad before as tonight when Catherine found him.

So he was not much of a catch, a broken man with a broken business which would shortly go back to the bank along with his house if he could not keep paying. Not that there was anything wrong with the business, just that the work and debt was slowly eating him up and it was beyond him to work if he could not sleep without dreaming nightmares, and then when he woke his body shook so much he could barely walk.

Catherine told him about her own life, her mother getting pregnant after being raped when fifteen, going first to Melbourne so that baby Catherine would not be taken away, then her mother having to work as a prostitute to feed them both, then having to run away again when the authorities in Melbourne wanted to take away her daughter. She told how her mother ran away again and came to Broome, of her being a little girl in Broome and being really happy with just her Mum and her friends as her mother made a success of her life, then the awful time when her Mum had run away again to the desert, how her car had broken down and they would have died of thirst until her childhood friend Sophie, whose room she stayed in now had come and rescued them.

As she spoke of Sophie she remembered the locket around her neck. She took it off and placed it in his palm with her own hands wrapped tightly around his. She told him to relax and feel her presence, dark eyed child of another time. She felt the tension flow out of him as she spoke, there was a three way presence of this other in her mind and Mathew's.

He nodded, "I am glad she was your friend and is now mine too. It is as if we both have a shared memory through her which lets light into our innermost parts and provides a path forward together.

She told of her life with the aborigines, then of her new father Robbie, how he and her Mum had really rescued each other from themselves and the loneliness and of how happy they now were together.

She even told him about going out with Richard the two times last week and of what her Grandmother had said after, "It is good to know what is not right, then you will know when the right one comes along."

So now she knew that she and Mathew were right together and that was all that mattered. Together they would make the business work. She told him that she had wanted to ask him about what course she should study and whether she could work part time to support herself. Now none of that mattered, maybe she would go to University later; for now she would work with him in the business until they got on top of their debts.

So by the end of the night it was agreed. They would get married as soon as it could be arranged and she would stay on with her Gran until then. After that they would live together in his house or maybe sell the house and fix up a room in the pub for a new home, it would be easier just to live there until it was making plenty of money.

In the early dawn they both fell into a deep sleep, and were only awoken when Ella came in to unlock for the day at ten o'clock. There heard her banging around out in the front, so Mathew went out to talk to her, to say he had fallen asleep on the couch.

As he came out Mathew saw Ella holding Catherine's handbag and pointing to a till full of money, with her eyes raised in a question. He found himself laughing, he could not keep a secret from her direct stare and he was too happy to lie.

He said, "Catherine is sleeping on the lounge. She found me out the back last night, curled up and shaking. She stayed with me for the night. She is the loveliest girl and we are going to get married."

Ella said, "Wow, that was fast. I could tell you both liked each other, but I would never have guessed that it would only take one day when it was just the two of you together before it happened. Still I am glad, really glad for you both.

"I have sometimes thought I should go into partnership with you in the pub, I know we could make it work. But my boyfriend would be too jealous and never agree. So I am really pleased she is the one. I think together you can make it work. I hope you will be happy together.

As she said this a bleary eyed Catherine walked out and came and put her arms around Mathew. Ella came over and they had a group hug.

Then Catherine said, "Maybe we should all be partners in making this pub work, I think that once we have cleared the debts there is plenty of money in it for us all to make a good living."

In a flash Catherine knew clearly what she would do, she could feel her mothers business brain kicking in along with all the little things her mother had taught her as a child; how to give others a share of the business and motivate them.

Ella looked at her strangely, "What do you mean?"

Catherine said, "Well my mother started her own business in Broome when she was fifteen, all on her own. By the time she was twenty one she owned three businesses and a warehouse with twenty staff. Those who had worked well for a couple years mostly shared the business profits. Her motto was a share for the business and a share for the workers.

"So I was thinking, you have worked hard to help Mathew make a success for a couple years, really it is you as much as him who has made it work so far. So perhaps we should formally give you a share, though of course it is not mine to give away but Mathew's, but then if we are going to get married I suppose it will be both of ours."

Mathew hugged her tight. "I can see why I want to marry you, it is that business brain I need."

So over a cup of coffee in the kitchen it was agreed. If she worked for them and only took the drawings the business could afford until the debts were under control, in return she would take a twenty percent share of the profits, on top of her regular wage from the end of the year. And, who knew, but if the business was doing well next year maybe it could cover her to buy a pub of her own, that was Ella's real ambition.

Mathew offered to write it out on a piece of paper. The other two shook their heads. "If we don't trust each other the paper is worthless. If we do we don't need the paper for now, later the bank and a solicitor can draw up whatever formal contracts we need."

Chapter 8 - Wedding

The wedding of Catherine Renshaw and Mathew Jamison was planned for the first week of April. It was to be held in the church at the top of the hill in Balmain, the church where Catherine and her Granny went and where Lizzie went as a child. For their honeymoon they were booked to go to Broome and out to the desert for a week to meet all Catherine's Aboriginal family and then to fly to Perth for a week where they stayed in a fancy hotel looking out over the Swan River, that was her Mum and Dad's wedding gift to them.

As well her parents sent a cheque for ten thousand dollars, saying it was also a wedding gift. Catherine was at first inclined to refuse the money. But Mathew, after a private chat to Robbie about Catherine's independence, 'just like Lizzie's', Robbie said, formed the view it was a good idea. So Mathew got Catherine's agreement that it be treated as a loan, paid back when the business was on more solid ground. It took the pressure off for the next few months and that was important for them both.

It all happened so fast. That morning they walked back to tell her Gran. Her Gran was not too surprised; it was funny how other people could see things one could not see. She said she had always liked Mathew since he was a boy and, with David gone away now, it was like getting another son back into her family, along with the added bonus of keeping her much loved Granddaughter nearby, so she was delighted. Her Gran said their difference in age was no one's business but their own. If it did not matter to them why should it matter to anyone else.

Her Mum and Dad were a bit surprised, after all they had never met this man, though his name had come up around the dinner table over their holidays a couple of times and they knew how his brother had been David's best friend at school. So it was not like he was unknown. In fact he was one of the boys around Lizzie's own age that she had known slightly as a child at school, but that was a life time ago.

When Cathy told her Mum he reminded her of her Dad, and she felt just the same way about him that Lizzie did about Robbie and vice versa, Lizzie knew there was no point arguing.

Two weeks after they made their announcement her Mum and Dad flew across for an engagement party held in the hotel and Lizzie had stayed for an extra week to help her Grandma plan the wedding though the other children stayed at school in Broome.

Once they met Mathew they both liked him at once and agreed that as they had made up their minds they might as well just go ahead and get married sooner rather than later. Robbie found he had a natural affinity for Mathew as someone who had served in combat and been injured.

So, a mere six weeks and four days after that night when Catherine and Mathew decided, the wedding bells were ringing.

Robbie felt so proud bringing Catherine on his arm to the front of the church; she was sparkling and radiant in her white wedding gown. She had Lizzie's intense eyes and searching look, but she had something all of her own, a more delicate look and a softness and roundness. Since first he had held her, he had felt enormous affection for this child.

He remembered that night when he had fallen in love with Lizzie, the first full night she had spent with him, only a couple weeks after they met. He remembered how Catherine, a tiny but perfect baby, lay sleeping in a crib in the corner of his room as he and Lizzie had loved each other in the night. He remembered how, in the early morning grey light, Cathy awoke making little baby sounds and Lizzie had stirred in her sleep, face beautiful with dark hair across the pillow. He could not bear to disturb her dream so he slid out of bed and took up this tiny child who had snuggled in to him, nuzzling with small gurgles as she searched for a breast.

So he had carried Catherine to the bed and placed her on her mother's breast while Lizzie barely stirred. He had watched, absorbed by her simple baby world, as she drunk greedily and then fell asleep. Then he had placed her tiny body between theirs as they lay sleeping in Melbourne all those many years ago.

Then he remembered her when he returned to Lizzie in the desert, this solemn eyed girl of six, his instant ally and friend. She had claimed, not without some truth, that she had arranged for his return. He remembered the delight he felt on that first day when she had called him Dad, he the adopted father of a child who had known no father, and on that day he had promised himself he would do anything he could to be the best father of this child who had taken him into her heart as much as her mother had.

As the years had gone by Catherine had alternated between calling him Robbie and Dad, but to this day she mostly called him Dad, and every time she did it warmed something at his core.

Now she was all grown up but still so young and vulnerable. Here she was marrying a man that she said reminded her of him, her adopted Dad. Robbie could understand why. Mathew was a bit broken inside the way he had been until he had returned to Lizzie, not to mention they both walked with a limp, his from a motorbike accident and a leg rebuilt with bits of steel, Mathew from a piece of metal that had smashed part of his hip.

So, while it was not the glittering life for Cathy that he may have imagined, he knew that she had found a good man who shared his love and affection for his daughter, Cathy. When Robbie saw Mathew look at her he remembered the love he had felt for Lizzie on the day they too had walked down the aisle of this same church. It was the love he still felt every time Lizzie smiled at him.

He knew they would try and make a good life together which was all that could be asked. So today he was glad for Catherine, as was Lizzie. Sometimes he felt that Catherine was too young for what she was taking on but, as Lizzie reminded him, she was only fifteen when she made a life on her own and, compared to her, Catherine was positively grown up.

The ceremony was over all too soon, and then it was a reception in the local hall next to the church. It was filled to overflowing with the good people of Balmain, Lizzie had organised this with her typical efficiency. They had all agreed not to have the typical formal reception, but instead to have something like a drop in centre wedding reception after they had been inundated with requests from the town's people to come and share a drink with their publican friend. It was hard to believe that so many people knew and liked Mathew. More than they could count offered to contribute towards an event where they could have a drink with him and give their well wishes, the local boy made good.

So, in the end, they decided that after the wedding service finished at about two o'clock, any friends who wanted could drop in for a drink and chat, with the service of copious food and drinks until 6 pm, when the immediate family would go for a small and intimate dinner.

It turned into a rowdy afternoon of good cheer as many came and went. A band played brackets of music from time to time and between people charged glasses, told stories of the Mathew they had known since a child of the streets, some added their own stories of Lizzie and other local identities, not to mention Patsy and other members of both families.

In the corner was a pile of presents, Lizzie had said she wanted no donations to the reception but those who wanted could leave a present for the couple, anything from a note and card to something more. Now a great pile filled the corner, bottles of spirits, household appliances, a wonderful old carved table and chairs, glasses, china, silverware, and so many cards, often with money folded inside. While no one had really been counting it seemed like three of four hundred people had come and gone as the afternoon unfolded and tomorrow they would need a truck to shift all the gifts. It was a wonderful celebration of the love of the town for one of its own; they took this couple to their hearts like a fairy tale story.

After they were married they stayed for three nights in the Intercontinental Hotel in Sydney before flying to Broome for their honeymoon with a night in Hotel Darwin. That night in Darwin they walked together around the town, down to the wharf with the boat wrecks still remaining from the bombing of the war, then back to the hotel where they shared a drink under the slow flap of the ceiling canvass fans.

Together in bed that night, Catherine traced the scarred outline of that wound on Mathew's hip and his hand lingered over the naked curves of her own rounded hips and breasts. She felt indescribably happy, as if her whole life had been waiting for this time and this man, he had made her wait until the wedding night for their bodies to join which had driven her mad at the time, but now she was so glad.

Since that night when she first held him the tremors had almost gone away, just odd flashes in his dreams and he told her she had only to touch him and they would go away. Now, with their bodies joined, she was convinced she could draw all the poison from him and take it harmlessly away, put into a place where it could harm neither of them anymore. Already she was wanting for him to make a child inside her, a perfect formed expression of their love in new life.

Chapter 9 - A Business Together

Two months later, back in Sydney, Catherine knew she was pregnant; she thought it must have happened on her honeymoon as she had skipped the period which was due three weeks after they were married. Now that over another month had gone by with still nothing, she was sure. She could feel the subtle changes that were happening inside her body, her nipples had enlarged and changed colour, her breasts were filling out and tingling, and sometimes in the morning she felt strangely unable to eat breakfast, though it always passed after an hour or two.

They were staying in Sophie's room in her Gran's place at the moment; they had sold the house in Rosser Street for a good price though the cheque was yet to come in. They had put the money from her Mum and Dad into building a two bedroom apartment for themselves in an upstairs corner of the hotel, having taking over three old and run down bedrooms, a lounge room previously used for paying guests and a bathroom. They were turning this space into their own place within the hotel. It had a door to the outside, down a rickety flight of backstairs and inside it would have a small kitchen dining room, a lounge room, a good sized bedroom for them and a second smaller bedroom which currently served as an office but which could become a child's room in due course. They were also blocking off part of the back yard of the hotel next to the stairs up to their place into a small private courtyard so they could sit outside in privacy if they wanted to.

She and Mathew had drawn up the plans together, using graph paper to get the scale and had given these to a draftsman to turn into proper plans. Now the builders were at work. It would be finished in two more weeks and then they would move into their new home, it was partly convenience and partly economy that he led to the decision to live on the premises, it would save time, allowing them to devote their full energies to building up the business and they both liked the idea of it being their own new home, the place where they had first met, not the continued family home of another generation.

And freeing up the money by selling the house in Rosser Street would allow them to do both some much needed refurbishment of the rest of the hotel and pay down their debts with the bank, enough to give them a cost buffer so they did not have to worry each month whether they could afford the repayments.

Catherine knew that, deep down, Mathew was a bit sad on the day his family house had sold. But he told her he had no regrets as they could now build a new life together, which was better than keeping memories. From the old house they had taken as much furniture as they could use along with old pictures and other memorabilia. That way Mathew's memories from that house and his past life could live on alongside the new ones they would create together.

Next month they would move into their own new apartment. Catherine loved her room and living with her Gran, and Mathew loved her Gran too, plus her food was fantastic, much better than Catherine's limited ability though she was now getting Gran to teach her some favourite dishes.

But she could barely wait until they would really start a new life together, just the two of them living in their own new place. By early next year, please God, they would have a third life in their family to add to their own. There was a simple goodness to their life together which reminded her of living with her aboriginal family and friends out in the desert.

Chapter 10 - A Perfect Child

Two weeks after New Year celebrations Catherine gave birth to a little girl in Balmain hospital. Despite the convention this was women's business she had insisted that Mathew was there to hold her hand during the labour, along with her Mum and Gran to add their own support. Mathew was the first to hold the baby, obviously nervous but very proud. After a few minutes, the baby was passed to Catherine to hold herself. She thought her little girl was just perfect, beautiful in every way, a bit of her, a bit of Mathew and a bit of something else which she could not identify, but the whole package was a new and wonderful person.

They had decided on the name Amelie, a French name which had been the name of an orphan girl in Vietnam who had attached herself to Mathew. At that time Mathew had promised himself if he ever had a girl child he would name it after this orphan waif, barely eight years old, who had befriended him and then been so cruelly killed. Somehow the name suited their baby perfectly, from the minute she opened her eyes and first looked at them she had something of the waif like free spirit to her nature that he had remembered and described when he told Catherine the story. Catherine had added Elizabeth as her middle name, so as to carry on her own Mum's name.

Mother and child came home to the hotel apartment after a week and life settled into an easy routine. They placed a cot next to their bed though for the first three months Amelie often cuddled into bed with them; it was easier to feed her that way at night as Catherine only had to roll to the side to give her a breast.

Catherine was surprised how naturally and effortlessly she had settled into motherhood, perhaps it was the sense of practicality she had gained from her own mother, she enjoyed her baby but the child was easy and she did not feel the need to fuss over her, instead she loved her and gave her attention and still found time for her other life in the hotel. It was good to live and work in the one place, because she could work in the bar and, in a minute, if her baby cried, she could be upstairs to attend to her.

So weeks and then months drifted by, soon it was autumn and then winter, and then it was back into spring. By now little Amelie was crawling around, they had blocked off the stairs with a baby proof gate at the top.

Amelie particularly loved her Daddy, she was always crawling up to him and putting up her arms to be picked up, sometimes Catherine complained that he spoiled the child rotten as he would always stop whatever he was doing to bring her up and bounce her on his lap, or carry her tucked into one arm as he worked with the other.

Amelie was very friendly and all the bar staff and the regular patrons clearly had a soft spot for her, though once the bar got busy after the mid-afternoon she was always confined to the upstairs to keep her away from people's feet. Now she was learning to stand up and pull herself around the furniture. When she wanted something she would crawl to the top of the stairs, pull herself up and shout out to those below, using her baby talk, until someone came to attend to her.

Her first birthday was planned as an occasion of local celebration, following just after the New Year festivities had passed and the town returned to its normal quieter pace. They decided to hold the party in the big courtyard in the back of the hotel. They invited all their staff, selected customers who had become family friends and some of their friends from the other small businesses from around Balmain, those who supplied services like the plumber and electrician and others who found time to pop in for a friendly chat and occasional drink.

Gran Patsy, Lizzie, Robbie and her brother and sister were not there as they had all gone to Melbourne this year to stay at Robbie's Mum's place for Christmas and now they were all back in Broome. But in two weeks' time Catherine and Mathew were flying to Broome for their first well deserved holiday since their marriage.

Catherine particularly wanted to take Amelie into the desert and introduce her to all her black aunts and uncles, let them give her the allotted skin name and incorporate her into her tribal family.

At the party Amelie ran around endlessly, like an unexploded missile, chasing other children and anything that took her fancy, barely stopping to eat, but with a smile which covered her whole face. She was full of chatter though the words were simple, Ma-ma-ma, Da-da-da-da, doggie-doggie, puddytat, me-me-me, Amelie.

Chapter 11 - A Busy Year

On returning from their holiday Catherine plunged herself back into work. She loved it but it was frenetic. After deciding for the last two years to defer her studies at University due to the need to get the pub back on its feet and also with a new baby, she found this year she really wanted to get on with this part of her life. She could also see how a business qualification would help, not only with their own business, but also with helping Ella get her own new business up and running.

By the end of the first year before Amelie was born the hotel was making a solid profit after all expenses. That year it had been a pleasure for her and Mathew to give Ella a big Christmas bonus out of the profit pool, and this along with the twenty percent of the profits that Ella was drawing from their business had meant that she was now in a strong position to look for a business of her own.

Ella had spent several months investigating a range of options, being mainly interested in something down the far end of Rozelle close to Victoria Road. The customers up there would be different and so it would take little business away from their hotel, but it was also close enough to share staff if desired, do joint promotions, combine orders, and get other efficiencies of having two businesses working in the same general area.

Finally she found the place that suited. They all visited for an inspection and agreed was just right. It needed a "freshen up" but that could happen in time, and it was in a good location with regular custom from the Iron Cove dockside. So they signed all the papers.

This time Cathy and Robbie's hotel had a 20% stake in Ella's business in return for providing a bank guarantee to cover her loan through their own business. After the first year when it was up and running and the guarantee was no longer needed they would then take a 20% share of the profits in the same way that Ella was taking her share from their business. In due course, if they wanted, they could exchange their shares, to give each party full ownership. At this stage they each liked the connection to the other that their share gave and the combined business structure seemed to be an overall benefit to both. But most of all they had become such close friends that it was nice to see each other regularly and do at least weekly shifts in each other's pubs.

Now that Catherine had got her teeth into business management she found an insatiable desire to know more and use this knowledge to build up and expand the business. She realized she was her mother's daughter. All her early life lessons about how to run a business that made a profit, looked after its workers and, with time, gained security through growth and good service, had become her own mantra as much as it had been her mother's before her.

So now she enrolled in a part time Commerce Degree which began at the start of March. With it she not only had a daughter to look after and a hotel to manage but lessons to go to and study and assignments to do when she came home. She loved it all but found there were just not enough hours in the day to get it all done, though she gave it her best shot.

Now they had an elderly lady, a local Grandmother, who came in two afternoons and evenings to mind Amelie from when the hotel became busy and Mathew was needed down stairs. As well as this Gran Patsy came one afternoon and evening to take a turn minding their child. She offered to do more but Cathy resisted, saying they wanted to see her lots but not just to do work for them, but rather to enjoy her company. So alternate weeks she came for Sunday evening dinner and the opposite weeks they went to her place for Sunday lunch. But these days, each Wednesday were her Gran's own time alone with her own great granddaughter both seemed to love this time and would often go off together, sometimes walking the town or going to a park, other times visiting other people her Gran knew.

Three nights a week Catherine had University and on those nights Mathew would eat a meal cooked in the restaurant and put Amelie to bed. Then when she got home she would peep in and, if Amelie was still awake, she cuddled into bed with her for a few minutes and told her a story.

More often than not she fell asleep alongside her until Mathew woke her when it was time for them both to come to bed. Then mostly she stumbled into their own bed and fell back into her dreams with barely a word exchanged. More often than not Amelie also came into bed with them at some stage so her kicking and moving about would then break up their sleep. So their love life suffered with Amelie sharing the bed and with her own tiredness, but she had promised Mathew that before long they would all go away together for a holiday and then she would make it up to him. They still had luxurious Sunday mornings to sleep in together and on waking refreshed to reconnect their bodies and minds. The rest of the time they just had to manage as best they could.

Chapter 12 - More Tremors

Eighteen months had passed since their baby was born and for Catherine it was hard to believe life could get any better. Sure it was busy, with a small child, now a toddler, who was always under her feet. That plus the business meant she was run off her feet most of the day, not to mention her study. But she was happy, unbelievably happy. She felt like her life had discovered a real purpose, their days were full, the business turnover had increased by a third in the past year and they were more than half way through paying their bank loan down to zero.

Ella and she continued as the best of friends. Ella was now talking about getting married to her own man, which was something that Cathy was unsure of, worried that he had a possessive edge that could turn to jealousy and even violence, but that was Ella's business.

But Ella's hotel was starting to make serious money and Ella still worked one or two nights a week here to keep in touch, the quiet nights at her own hotel when her regular bar manager could cover it on his own. On one of those nights each week Cathy, Mathew and Ella would share the bar work along with doing their joint books as it gave a good chance for them all to keep across both businesses. Ella was now taking a regular wage out of the other business and combined with the twenty percent of the profits from this place she had a useful pool of her own money to put back into her own pub, which was now being gradually refurbished, one room at a time, so it did not affect turnover.

Cathy had worked out they could even look at getting a third place, a joint venture between their business and Ella's if they wanted. She was undecided, Ella was keen, but Mathew was more cautious, knowing how close he had come to the wall before Cathy had come into his life.

But she and Ella had done the sums and worked out that with the extra turnover the two places were generating they could let the debt go up by half, using this money to establish the third business. They could still cover repayments comfortably on this increased debt from the takings of the first two hotels while the next one got going. In the end, after Mathew had gone carefully through all the figures which she and Ella had worked up, he gave qualified agreement; "only for the right place at the right price which we all like." So when that right place was found it would go ahead.

Toddler Amelie was delightful, a chattering ball of activity, trouble with a capital T. She had everyone charmed, the customers, the staff, their friends. Mathew sometimes complained that she had so many aunts and uncles she barely knew he was her father, though she always knew who was her mother. But it was good humoured banter and, when Amelie sat on his lap, pulling his hair and chanting "Da, Da, Da," Catherine could see he was as happy as she.

One night in July, a cold night, they decided to try Amelia in her own room for the whole night. They wanted the more peaceful sleep that came when she did not spend half the night in their bed kicking them. Their love life had suffered a lot in the last few months from a third person in the bed and Cathy was feeling it was time to try for a second baby, not that she did not have enough else going on in her life, but she loved being a mother as well and she loved the mind image of herself and Mathew with a whole tribe of kids.

Since Amelie had been fully weaned, six months ago, she had expected to fall pregnant, but not so far. They both had to admit that coming to bed late and tired often meant they just fell asleep, so perhaps they had not managed to get the timing to coincide with her fertile period, at least not just yet.

But she felt ready now for another baby, in fact she would not mind twins, now that her life was getting settled into a comfortable though busy routine. So tonight they had both agreed that they would ignore any grizzling and crying from Amelie for at least half an hour before they gave in to her and let her come in with them.

Their lovemaking was wonderful and it felt so good to fall asleep just cuddling each other without a baby pushing in. Catherine fell into a deep and dreamless sleep. She awoke to noise and movement. She realised Mathew was tossing restlessly and talking in his sleep, muttering the words "No, No, No," and shaking his head. She pushed her body into his and, when he did not settle, she woke him up. He looked at her blearily.

You were dreaming she said, it must have been one of those bad dreams because you kept saying the words, "No, No, No."

He said, "I don't remember anything. It is ages since I remember a bad dream, not since I started sharing my nights with you."

There was a muted light from the street coming in the window from a gap in the curtains. He was between her and the window, in the shadows. The light was shining on her skin, glowing faint, luminous white where the covers had come off leaving her naked body exposed.

She felt his eyes turn to her, looking intently at her body in the soft light. She felt exposed and vulnerable in this light. But she could feel the sight of her body arousing him, and she loved the hard feeling as he pushed his body over and into hers. Now all false modesty vanished in the physical contact of their lovemaking. Later, as he returned to sleep, she lay there stroking his hair in the soft light feeling so replete with their passion. Her body felt very ripe tonight and she wondered if he had just created a new life within her. It was a wonderful thought. She fell asleep again and did not wake until bright winter sunlight was streaming into the room.

A week passed and then another with life continuing on its peaceful path. It was now August and the late winter flowers were starting to show, the cherry tree behind the hotel was a mass of buds, the promise of new life. She was almost certain that there was a new life growing inside her. Not that anything was showing and her periods were barely overdue, but a sixth sense said it was so.

Mathew had a couple more bad dreams in fact, if she thought about it, they were probably happening most nights and each was similar to the first. They had passed in the same way as the first and each dream was followed by more waking lovemaking so it was almost pleasure to wake him in anticipation of what followed. Yet the pattern was strangely disturbing to her, as if a beast inside him refused to stay quiet and was now waking.

Another two weeks passed. Now she was really sure she was pregnant. She told Mathew and Ella. Both professed delight, though Mathew did qualify it with. "You are busy enough with one child, how will you go with two and still have time for me. I fear our lovemaking will again be the casualty."

She knew it was good humoured banter, but yet there was an edge to it she had not heard before. She hugged herself to him, "Oh Mathew, there will always be time for you. You are the centre of my life, the one who brings me the most joy and makes it all worthwhile."

He hugged her back. "I know; it is just all too perfect. Sometimes I think we have got too busy to stop and smell the roses. Sometimes I think there must be a shadow in the deep waiting to come and spoil it."

She refused to countenance anything that could shatter this perfection. Yes, she was often so frenetically busy and would come to bed tired. But her mind was so full of good ideas that she just could not let go and these had to be acted upon before they vanished. It would be fine.

A month later she was tidying away at the bar, mid-afternoon, alone by herself. Amelie was sleeping in the bedroom, Mathew out collecting orders and Ella was inspecting another hotel that may be suitable. Only three customers were in the bar, sitting in a corner table.

She started to feel twinges of discomfort in her lower belly. She wondered if she had eaten something bad for lunch, it was like a low grade tummy upset. But then, as she thought more about it, she realised it had been there for a couple days and she had been ignoring it. She remembered this morning, holding a struggling Amelie as she had kicked hard against her belly and it had hurt, hurt a lot. Perhaps it was that, the kick, but she did not think so. She was almost sure it had been there, just at the edge of her awareness for a couple days now.

In a flash, a violent surge of pain swept over her. Her hands went to her belly; it hurt so much she could barely breathe as if she was buried under a huge pain wave which would drown her. It eased off a bit, and she straightened, supporting herself against the bar.

She realised she must have groaned out loud, the three men in the corner table were gazing at her with concern.

One spoke out, "You OK, love?"

She was about to say, "Yes fine," when another, even more violent, pain spasm gripped her. She heard herself cry out; she could not stand and she fell to the floor. She heard the sound of running feet but was lost in a world of pain.

One of the men from the corner was standing over her, reaching down for her, looking uncertain. The pain began to recede, she found her voice, "I think it is passing now, but would you ring for a doctor please."

Two of the men took her arms, one at each side and led her to a lounge chair against the wall. They eased her in, half sitting, half slumped. The pain was coming in waves now, so severe she could barely breathe. Each time she would make little cries that she could not stop. Then it would ease off and she could draw a few breaths before it returned.

She heard one of the men saying that an ambulance was on its way. She asked one man to go up to the bedroom and bring down Amelie; she would have to come with her to hospital as she could not be left alone in her room. Then two ambulance officers were in the room, loading her onto a stretcher.

The man returned with her crying baby, unhappy to be woken from sleep. She told the ambulance officers, when she could speak between bursts of pain, that her baby needed to come with her. She tried to comfort Amelie, but it was beyond her, as each time the pain came she would cry out. In the end she asked the man who seemed to be having the most success calming Amelie to come with her in the ambulance to hospital while the others stayed to let Mathew know.

She felt a prick in her thigh as one of the ambulance officers gave her a needle to ease the pain. Gradually it faded into a more blurry place. She realised they were driving through the town. Then she recognised that they were wheeling her into the Emergency Department of Prince Alfred Hospital. Then doctors and nurses were checking her, poking and prodding and discussing what it could be and the tests the needed to run.

Now it was off to the X-ray Department to try and take a picture of her belly, see whether she had gall stones or some other cause. Somewhere during it all she was joined by Mathew, now holding Amelie, his face white with worry. They had connected her to a drip now with a morphine infusion so it was hard to think straight but the pain was still there. At last, X-rays done, she realised they were talking about her with Mathew and discussing what they should do.

The gist of it was there was something significantly wrong in her lower abdomen, probably not gall stones, but kidney or bladder stones were possible. They also knew she was pregnant and said it could be something to do with this, or maybe acute appendicitis. Because the pain was so severe and they could not get a definite diagnosis from the other tests they were now saying they needed to do an exploratory laparotomy, to cut her belly open, to find and fix the problem.

She did not like the sound of it but realised they had no choice; the pain had to be fixed. She nodded, showing she agreed, and Mathew signed a consent form. They gave her another injection to make her even more sleepy. Soon she was given a mask of a funny smelling gas to make her go to fully to sleep. That was when her memory stopped.

She woke up feeling like her head was full of cotton wool. There was a diffuse pain across the bottom of her belly but the sharp pain was gone. She pushed her eyelids open, she felt incredibly tired.

Mathew was sitting beside her bed, looking at her with a mix of affection and worry. She caught his eyes and managed a smile which he returned.

He took her hand. "It is so good to see you awake and smiling. I have been worried sick about you, though the surgeon and the other doctors kept trying to assure me that you would be alright. Now that your eyes are open and I see your smile I can believe them. How do you feel?"

"Like my head is full of cotton wool and the bottom of my tummy is still hurting, but at least the sharp pain has gone," she replied. "Can you tell me what happened, was it something about the baby. Did I have a miscarriage?"

Mathew looked at her seriously and nodded. "Yes it was about the baby, something like what you said, not a miscarriage but something similar. I don't quite understand. They said it was an ectopic pregnancy, the baby was growing in the wrong place, at the very top of what they called your tube and it had died, so they had to operate and take it out, as well at ovary and that part of your tube. But they say you should still be able to have other babies from your other ovary as that side is normal.

"I don't care about that, I just care that you are OK, they said it had just burst when they took you to theatre and you had a big bleed, and for a while it was touch and go. I could not bear to lose you. You mean the whole world to me."

As it sunk in Catherine felt an awful empty feeling, she had a new life before which she had loved growing inside her and now it was gone. She knew it was tiny and she had not really known it, yet she felt unbelievably sad that it was gone without her ever knowing this person. She could feel tears running down her cheeks.

She put out her arms like a baby, wanting to be comforted, and Mathew enclosed her in an embrace, stroking her hair and murmuring words to her like she had to him when they first come together. The terrible ache of loss remained but she felt comforted.

She looked up and asked, "Where is Amelie?"

He answered. "I asked your Grandmother to take her home and mind her. They had to take you back to theatre a second time to stop the bleeding. So it is hours since you came here. Amelie and your Gran both stayed with you and me until about an hour ago, but it was getting very late and Amelie was tired and cranky. So, once the surgeon had finished and they brought you into recovery and we all knew you would be OK, I asked Patsy if she would take Amelie home and care for her this evening and I would ring later once you woke up properly.

Catherine nodded, she felt drained now that she knew the story; she felt sad and too tired to think. She kept hold of Mathew's hand saying, "Thank you for telling me. I am so tired I don't think I can stay awake much longer. But please stay with me. I don't want to be by myself tonight."

He nodded, "Of course, I had never dreamed of leaving until you were better, so tonight I will mind you, just the same as you once minded me."

She smiled a little smile and fell into a deep sleep. He sat holding her hand as the clock's hands moved slowly through the night. A couple times she half woke. Each time when she looked up and saw him sitting there she smiled and drifted back to sleep.

Mathew was tired but did not care; he knew he had almost lost her today. He was going nowhere without her and was determined to mind her better from here on.

Chapter 13 - Beginning Again

In the morning when Catherine woke up she saw Mathew was sleeping. His body was sitting on the bedside chair bed with his head slumped on the bed and touching her side. She fondly ran her fingers through his hair. She felt weak and tired but mostly glad to see him, to know he was still here and sleeping beside her. She could not wait to see her daughter again as well, her bright smile and her bubbling chatter.

There was a hole inside her from her loss, but she knew it was a small thing besides what she had, her husband and daughter who loved her as much as she loved them, and a solid family as well, all of whom she loved and loved her in equal measure.

In this place she saw clearly now that the life she still had was a gift that must never be wasted. It was no great insight, just an everyday appreciation, but she knew it was something she must never lose sight of.

As she idly stroked Mathew's hair she saw his eyes begin to flicker and then he was awake, looking at her dreamily. "I just had the most beautiful dream," he said, "It was about you and how much I loved you and how lucky I am."

"I was thinking just the same. "Thank you for staying all night with me, in that uncomfortable chair."

It was four days until she was able to get up and walk around and another day until they let her out of hospital. Her tummy was still tender where they had cut her and stitched her back up but it was healing well, and she was still pasty and weak on her feet from the blood loss. But she was recovering well. For the next week after she was home she was under strict doctors instructions to rest up, no sudden jerks of movements which might tear her stitches. It made her be patient, which was hard once she felt better, but it gave her time to think.

She realised she had started to let the business of her life consume her, trying to do so much to make a success of the business that some of the good things in her life were in danger of slipping away. But it was her warning she would heed it and slow down a bit, make sure there was more time for Mathew and Amelie, not be in such a desperate hurry to both get the business making lots of money while trying to have another baby at the same time, instead she must fully enjoy what she had now.

She remembered the story Lizzie had told her of how her own Mum, Patsy, had been desperate to have another baby and had started to forget about the child and husband she had already and what a high price had been paid for that. Not that this person that Lizzie had told her about seemed at all like her Gran now, she was so wise and patient, but then that character had of course come at a huge cost.

She was determined to try and learn her lesson without causing more harm. So she forced herself to slow down, they organised picnics at the weekend, often just the three of time at the beach or the park, sometimes with her Gran or others they knew, particularly those with their own small children. She finished painting their rooms, she bought furnishings that she and Mathew chose together to make their place nice, she tried to make sure they ate dinner at a regular hour and there was always good food on hand, she pampered her husband in lots of little ways.

But as time went by it was hard to maintain their slow and relaxed life, now Ella's own hotel was getting busier and busier and there was so much to do at this one. And Mathew had insisted that she not abandon her studies, he said she was way too bright to waste her brain on just being a hotel manager or his wife. So, even though she had dropped the studies for the rest of this year once she had lost her baby, from next year she would continue her part time course at University.

The year went by and then it was into the second year. Now Amelie was almost three and Christmas was coming. All Catherine's family was flying to Sydney for the Christmas holidays and she was so looking forward to seeing them all, her brother and sister were starting to sound so grown up when they talked on the phone, her brother Michael was now fifteen and her sister Emily was twelve. Soon they would be sent off to school too, though now her parents were talking of moving to a big city to live while the other children finished school, perhaps Perth, or even Sydney or Melbourne. She did not want that as it would break the link with her desert home, but it was not really up to her.

Christmas came round and it was wonderful, the first year Amelie really knew what presents were and everyone had spoilt her rotten. Her father had bought her a red car with pedals, *a strange present for a girl*, Catherine thought. Mathew said he had always wanted a car just like that when he was really little, because one of his friends had one and he would only let him drive it sometimes. So now the red car had been hidden away in the cupboard until Christmas morning, well almost.

Three nights before Christmas, after Amelie was supposed to be asleep in her bed, with Cathy's mother, father, brother and sister all sitting round in their apartment. Mathew had brought out the car to show everyone. He could not help it because he loved it so much himself, shiny red with flashing headlights.

As they were all sitting round and admiring it a little voice came from behind. "Car, Red Car." There was Amelie, standing in the door, eyes wide open and looking rapturously at the car. She toddled over and, without a second glance at anyone, climbed in and started to pedal, whooping with delight. Mathew covered his face with pretend horror that he had not closed her bedroom door properly.

But there was no undoing it, she loved her car.

Once she was back in bed the car went back into the cupboard, hidden out of sight.

Amelie came running out first thing next morning looking, "Car, Car, Red Car, Where Car? Car Gone. Where Car Gone?"

Mathew and Cathy pretended not to notice. After a long while of her walking around and looking everywhere Amelie finally gave a defeated shrug and said. "Car Gone."

On Christmas morning there was a huge object, wrapped in paper, sitting under the tree. At first Amelie did not want to go near it, as if scared it would bite her. Instead she opened and played with her other presents, "Santy brought me dolly, Santy brought me dress."

Mathew brought her to the car. He asked "Who is this present for?"

She shook her head, not knowing.

He found the card on it with her name, "It says Amelie, I wonder who Amelie is?

She pointed to herself, still looked uncertain.

"What do you think it is?" he asked.

She shook her head.

He asked, "Do you want to open it."

She shook her head again.

He lifted her right next to it and put her hand on it.

She looked nervous as if she wanted to pull her hand back. But then something curious must have tripped in her brain. She started to feel it intently. "Car," she said. Now she was tearing off the paper. Then, "Red Car, Santy bring back Red Car."

Beaming delight Amelie tore free the wrappings and climbed inside.

Now she would not get out, it was so precious and she was scared it might disappear again. She ate her breakfast sitting in it and when it came time to get dressed and go to church, she had to be pried, crying and holding tightly to the steering wheel, out of it.

When she came home, after church, she was so delighted that the car was still there. After that it became like the new house she lived in, though now she came and went secure in the knowledge it would not vanish again.

As Catherine thought back on it on New Year's Eve, she knew that this was one of the most wonderful times in her life which she must never forget. She now had a photo of Amelie sitting proudly in her red car. It sat in pride of place on their mantel piece. She made herself a promise that she would try to make the next year the best year of all their lives.

Chapter 14 - The Birthday Girl

January 14th was Amelie's 3rd birthday and all the family had stayed on in Sydney for the occasion.

It was still hard to separate her from her car, so, as a present, Mathew and Robbie, with help from Michael, built her a house, like an oversize dolls house. It was big enough for her to drive the car into and park inside. It had a front door that looked like a real house door but was six inches taller than she was. So she could walk through it without banging her head, and it was wide enough to drive the car in and out with a few inches to spare. The top level was like a regular dolls house with places for dolls furniture and with doll sized doors and windows which opened and shut and which she could reach from her bed.

The three of them had worked for many hours over the last week to create all the pieces, then assemble them to test that they fitted together. After that they pulled them all apart and painted them in bright colours. During the night, as Amelie lay sleeping, they carefully assembled it in the lounge room and carried it into the bedroom; it had only just fitted through the door.

They had part covered it in wrapping paper, so it was clear it was a present and put the car inside the underneath, but left the door open enough so that when she woke up she could see it was inside. They had all come over for early breakfast, no one wanting to miss the moment of discovery. They sat quietly in the kitchen, drinking cups of tea and waiting for Amelie to wake.

She normally woke about seven in the morning so they were there in good time and just starting on a second cup when the patter of little feet was heard. Silence, then the sound of paper tearing, then "House,

Car House, Santy Bring House for Car, Mummy and Daddy, Santy Bring House for Car."

They all trooped in and watched her drive the car in and out of the house, beaming with delight.

At 3 pm there was a party with four of her friends in the local park down at East Balmain with a view out to the Harbour Bridge. Michael and Emily were the stars of the party, given the job of entertaining two other little girls and two little boys all around Amelie's age that she knew from playgroup. They set up a splash pool and a bouncing castle full of air for the children to play on. After that there were lots of lollies and drinks and a birthday cake with two big candles which Amelie blew out, one at a time. The adults, including the other parents and a few close friends, stood around sipping champagne and beer and enjoying the view on a perfect summer's day as boats in the harbour drifted past their view and the ferries came and went.

When they carried Amelie home in the dusk she was so tired she could barely walk but said, "Mummy and Daddy, thank you for best, best bird day party."

Chapter 15 - Lumps

Next day Amelie was really tired and slept in until mid-morning. Catherine was not surprised after the huge day she had had yesterday. Most of the family had gone fishing on the harbour; it had become something of an annual event as they had done it last year too when they had gone on a holiday to Broome.

Robbie and Mathew had both loved to fish as kids and so today they had taken Emily and Michael out in a fishing boat, trying various spots around the harbour where Mathew had fished with his own father when little. Patsy had gone along too as she loved going out and about and also having time alone with her other grandchildren. So it was just her and her mother at home.

Catherine was secretly pleased. She had been so close to her Mum when she was little, she the only child of a single parent. While it was lovely to have everyone around, sometimes she just wanted time alone with her Mum. So far these holidays there had not been much of that.

They sat around the kitchen table eating slices of toast and honey and drinking endless cups of tea as they chatted and the morning drifted by. By about ten o'clock, with Amelie still sleeping, Catherine decided it was time to wake her, as the two of them wanted to walk down town and do some shopping and then have lunch together in an outdoor café.

She went in to look at her daughter, she was still sleeping soundly. She stroked her tousled hair, strangely reluctant to disturb her beautiful sleep. She saw Amelie had little discoloured blotches on the skin of her cheeks, she looked at them more closely, she supposed they were just from the inevitable summer stings and mozzie bites that were inflicted on them all, particularly Amelie, where all the bites still came up in lumps. She smoothed her hair back to look better, they were a funny colour for bites, she pushed back her lip and looked at the baby gums; they were a funny colour too and had bruised looking places, like bloodspots, on them here and there. It did not seem right.

She called in her Mum and showed her.

Lizzie looked closely, uncertain too.

Now Amelie was stirring, she sat up and rubbed her eyes sleepily. "Mummy I feel a bit sick," she said.

Catherine picked her up, she noticed there were little lumps under her arms, she could not remember them being there yesterday, but come to think of it for the last couple days she had barely held her little girl, there were so many helpers.

Perhaps she was coming down with one of those common children's complaints, like chicken pox or mumps, she recalled that mumps caused lumps under the chin and arms and seemed to recall that other kids sicknesses did the same, it was something about lymph glands there reacting and getting enlarged. Perhaps that was it; she was coming down with something like that.

She did seem a bit flushed this morning. She cuddled Amelie to her, she did not feel like she was running a temperature but it was hard to tell, she was still warm from her bed.

Catherine said to her Mum, "Will you have a look at this, she seems to have lumps under her arms, perhaps she is coming down with something, like chicken pox or mumps."

Her Mum took Amelie and felt under her arms then around her neck, nodding, "Yes definitely she seems to have enlarged glands, probably as you say a virus. I think they vaccinate for mumps these days so probably not that, but there are lots of other things they get when they are little.

"Anyway let's give her breakfast, see how she is, perhaps a quiet day is in order. If she does not spark up we should take her to the doctor."

Amelie did not eat much breakfast and after she said she was tired again so Catherine put her back to bed and suggested her Mum go for a walk down the street and bring back something for lunch.

An hour later Lizzie was back, carrying a couple containers of delicious smelling Chinese food for them to share. The aroma wafted through the apartment and woke Amelie who sat up on a stool and joined them in the meal. At first she seemed to eat well but about half way through she said. "Mummy, I feel sick again."

Lizzie looked up, "Time for a doctor's visit I think."

Catherine nodded and went and picked up the phone. She got an appointment in an hour's time. It was only a hundred yards walk down the street so the two of them went together, Lizzie carrying a shopping basket to buy some food for dinner while Catherine carried Amelie. After a few minutes wait the doctor, a pleasant young man, invited them in.

They gave him a brief history, saying maybe she had a kid's bug.

He asked a few questions, how long she had been showing signs and any other symptoms? Then he lifted Amelie onto the table to examine her. As he carefully looked over Amelie his demeanour changed from casual to worried looking. He was very thorough and checked everything over and then he went over her a second time, looking particularly carefully in her mouth, as well as palpating the glands all over her body. This time he was writing notes as he went, keeping his face fixed on the page until he was finished before he looked up.

He tried to smile, but there was no hiding the anxiety in his manner.

Catherine could feel her heart pounding, *What could it be? Amelie had seemed so well yesterday. But of course the excitement of a birthday for a three year old made that hardly surprising. Come to think of it though, she had not eaten much, though she had put that down to the excitement of the day.*

The doctor seemed to be gathering his thoughts and his words. "I am concerned about your daughter; it could be, as you say, a virus like chicken pox or mumps, though she has had her shots. But there are other things, symptoms like the blotches on her gums and she has enlarged white tonsils which do not really fit. So, I would like to take some blood and do some tests before we go any further, if that is OK. I most want to see what her white blood cell count is. That will help me know what to do next."

Catherine could feel panic rising, she did not like the ominous way he was speaking. It was his manner more than his words that set the alarm bells ringing. She tried to ask what it could be.

But the doctor, while not exactly refusing to answer, said. "I would really like to get the results of the blood test before we discuss what could be the problem."

So he arranged for a nurse to come in and take a blood sample. The nurse gave Amelie a lolly to suck and asked Catherine hold her tight while she did her job. Lizzie pulled funny faces to make her laugh and that helped. Amelie cried a little from the needle, but then she was very proud when they put a band-aid on her arm and told her how brave she was.

The doctor said he would look at a blood smear this afternoon and he should have the rest of the results by tomorrow, saying, "I will telephone you when I have looked this afternoon. It should be about half past five."

Catherine felt sick with worry and she could tell from the strain on her mother's face that Lizzie was feeling something similar. They decided they would treat Amelie to an ice-cream, a treat for being so brave. Now she was jumping with delight as if nothing could possibly be the matter. They both agreed that she suddenly did not look sick at all, but somehow neither believed she was magically better. They both tried to block the anxiety from their minds but it was no use.

Catherine finally said, "Oh Mum, there is something about the way that the doctor talked, after he looked at Amelie, that makes me feel sick to the bottom of my stomach, I am just so, so scared."

Her Mum said nothing but came and hugged her tightly, saying, "We have got through bad things together before. So now, whatever it is, we have to do the same. We must try and help each other be brave."

Catherine nodded, feeling tears prick her eyes. They walked aimlessly along the street for a while and ended up taking Amelie to the park down near the school where there were some swings and roundabouts and a few other little children, as it gave something to distract Amelie and keep them from their worry.

Now Amelie was yawning and looking tired again so they brought her home and tucked her into bed. There was no protest and that was also unusual, she rarely went to bed willingly.

In Catherine the sinking feeling grew even stronger. She just knew there was something seriously wrong with her little girl though she had no idea what it could be and could not bear to even let herself think about it. So she sat on her bed, in a mind numbed state, until finally a noise from downstairs alerted her that the others were home.

They had a great day out fishing and carried a booty of several fish they all proudly displayed. It was only after five minutes that Mathew said, "Where is my little girl?"

Catherine found herself unable to speak, she looked at Mathew with imploring eyes as if wishing she could stop him from knowing and at the same time hoping she could make it all alright.

Finally Lizzie spoke, rescuing the silence. "She is sick and sleeping. We are both quite worried about her. We took her to the doctor after lunch."

Mathew frowned and looked puzzled, "But she was bright as a button and so full of life yesterday. How can it be something too bad, or if it is she should be in hospital. Tell me what happened."

Now Catherine found her voice, knowing that it was up to her to explain. "When we took her to the doctor I thought she might be coming down with chicken pox or mumps of something like that. She was very tired this morning and did not want to eat. Then I saw funny blotches on her skin and gums and she had lumps under her arms.

"So we took her to the doctor, thinking he would say she was just coming down with a virus. At first, when he looked at her, it was like he thought that too. But then, as he looked more closely, you could see his manner change. You could tell he was worried too, he took some blood to do some tests, and said he should have some first results about five thirty.

"I have been thinking since that if it is not clear what the problem is maybe we should bring her up to hospital where they can treat her with antibiotics and fluids and things like that.

"After we brought her to the doctor we gave her an ice cream which she ate happily and then we took her to play in the park. But after a little while you could tell she was tired and so I brought her home and put her back to bed and she has stayed there ever since. I was sitting in there with her when you came home and she stayed fast asleep. It is amazing that she has not woken up with all the noise."

As she finished speaking she heard a little noise. There was Amelie standing at the door with her arms up. "Mummy and Daddy I feel sick."

Mathew was closest and scooped her up in his arms. The way he hugged her, so tenderly, almost brought tears to Catherine's eyes.

Please God, she prayed in her mind, *let my little girl be OK, not just for her sake but for mine and most of all for Mathew's. He loves her so much and I can not bear it for him if anything bad was to happen to her.*

It was like she could suddenly see this huge shadow sitting, not just over her but over him as well.

At that moment the phone in the hall rang, starting them all. It was only just coming up to five o'clock and seemed too early.

Mathew handed Amelie to Catherine and went to pick up the phone. She realised it was the doctor as Mathew spoke, "Hello Doctor Roberts, Yes it is Mathew here. My wife, Catherine, brought our little girl, Amelie, to you today to look at. Do you have some results of the tests?"

There was silence, all they could do was watch Mathew's face, and slowly a glassy and shocked look came over it as he listened. Finally he put down the phone, saying, "Yes we will do that straight away."

Catherine tried to connect with his eyes but all she could see was shock in them. She asked, "What did he say?"

Mathew shook his head, as if trying to clear his own thoughts enough to speak. "Well, he did not say anything specific really; again it was what he did not say.

"He said he has some initial blood results and they are of very serious concern and he would like us to both bring Amelie down to the hospital where he will meet us. He has arranged for a specialist and him to meet us there at half past five, so the specialist can examine Amelie too and give his own opinion. He also said he thinks it will be best if Amelie comes into hospital tonight as they need to do a lot more tests in the morning. So I said we will be there then to meet them both."

There was a stunned silence. No-one quite knew what to say.

Finally Lizzie spoke. "Do you want us to come with you or would you prefer to go on your own?"

Catherine breathed deeply to calm her racing heart and finally said. "Perhaps it would be best if just Mathew and I went, too many of us will get in the way. The rest of you are probably best to go home to Gran's. We will ring you when we have some more news.

Lizzie nodded. "Of course." She started to pack up and tidy away the things, saying, "Perhaps you should pack some clothes and toys for our little girl, I just wish we could bring her car in with her too as that would make her happiest, perhaps even the dolls' house as well."

That made everyone laugh, even Mathew, and broke the tension.

Catherine passed Amelie back to Mathew. "Perhaps you could see if she needs to go to the toilet and wash the ice cream off her face and I will pack some things for her," she said.

He nodded.

Amelie wriggled free of his arms, "Daddy put down to go to toilet, big girl now."

Mathew nodded and followed her down the hall.

Chapter 16 - The Dreaded Word

When they arrived at the hospital they were shown into a private room where two people sat, conferring in low voices.

Mathew led the way in, Catherine with Amelie in her arms following. There were brief introductions, Mathew to Dr Roberts and them both to Dr McPherson, the specialist.

Mathew turned to Dr Roberts and said. "Please, we need to know why you are so concerned. I am happy to have a second opinion but first we need to know what it is about."

Catherine could see Dr Roberts did not want to say, but knew he must. He looked away at the specialist, he looked at her and then back at the specialist. Finally he looked at them both, composed himself, took a deep breath and said. "After I finished seeing patients this afternoon I did a blood smear of your daughter's blood. It fitted with my worst fears. What I saw was huge numbers of white cells in the smear and lots of them are abnormal. I am afraid I think your daughter has leukaemia; that is cancer of the white blood cells."

Catherine saw Mathew sway as if hit by a passing truck. The doctor grabbed his arm to steady him. Mathew spoke back, "But Doctor, how can that be, we have a beautiful little girl who only yesterday had her third birthday party. She ran around and danced like a crazy thing, there was no stopping her. Today you are telling us she is sick with an awful disease that could kill her. It just does not make sense."

Now the specialist took over, "Mr and Mrs Jamison. I think it would be best if we all sat down and tried to talk this through. But first I would like to examine your daughter myself and confirm my colleague's findings."

They both nodded.

The man had a friendly smile and his manner was somehow reassuring, despite the awful news. He turned to Amelie and said. "I was hoping you would come and sit on my lap for a minute and open your mouth nice and wide so I can have a look inside."

Amelie nodded, she too seemed to trust this man.

Catherine passed her across to Dr McPherson and he pulled out a little toy, one of those snow displays where you shake it up and all the snow comes drifting down over the people and houses. He shook it and showed it to Amelie and she looked with wide eyes.

He said, "If you are really good and let me have a careful look at you, in your mouth and under your arms, you can keep that for tonight. Would you like that?

Amelie nodded enthusiastically. So she sat still for five minutes and he examined her carefully. Then he lifted her onto her own seat and gave her the promised toy. She sat there shaking it and watching the snow fall, lost in her own child's world of imagining. It was somehow comforting to Mathew and Catherine to see her so absorbed.

Then the Dr McPherson turned to them and said. "I am sure this is very frightening for you. That is why Doctor Roberts asked me to come in and try and explain it to you, to help you understand what it means. It does not necessarily have to be as bad as the L or C words sound.

"These days, with early treatment, most children your daughter's age do get better. It is hard for us all but I do not want you to lose hope, there is a good chance if we get the treatment underway quickly that Amelie will make a full recovery. I cannot promise you this but the chances are in our favour, seeing you have picked it up so early when she is barely showing signs of being sick."

They forced themselves to listen and try to understand. The two doctors showed them Amelie's blood smear and then a normal blood smear. They pointed out the normal white blood cells called lymphocytes which were just seen occasionally in the normal blood smear. Then they showed them their daughter's blood smear. Here were lots and lots more of these lymphocytes, including ones with different centres which they called lymphoblasts. They said these were the cancer cells, which were being produced in large numbers in the bone marrow, and were now spilling out into her blood and also forming lumps in her lymph glands.

Then the doctors explained that tomorrow they would do a full blood count, X-Rays and a range of other tests and, once they knew fully what they were dealing with, they would start treatment. The first treatment would be a medicine in a drip that they would run into her. It was a drug to kill the bad cells in her blood and bone marrow. It may make her hair fall out, and it would make her feel sick for a few days but its purpose was to kill all the cancer cells. It would involve two drugs given over about a week and then Amelie would have to spend a couple weeks in hospital under close observation to ensure that the cancer cells went away and her normal bone marrow cells recovered.

After that they expected Amelie would get much better. Then she a second treatment about a month later followed by regular checks to make sure the bad cells did not come back into her blood or bone marrow again.

Finally the specialist said. "You do not really have to leave her here tonight you know. If she would be happier at home with you, then you can bring her home and just bring her back for the tests in the morning. In fact until she begins treatment she can stay at home, treatment won't begin for two or three days yet, not until all the other test results are in.

Amelie seemed to understand the words "go home", she was nodding enthusiastically to that. As they were leaving Catherine said to Dr Roberts, Could you ring my mother, Lizzie, and explain to her what you said to me, she and my father and my Gran will want to know, and you can explain it much better than me. I want to take my little girl home now. She wrote the phone number down.

Mathew nodded, then said, "Please do that and thank you from both of us for telling us the truth."

The doctor's both nodded; there was no more to say.

So they brought Amelie home and sat her with them on the lounge, all watching television together. Neither Catherine nor Mathew felt they could eat, but they made up dinner for Amelie and took turns feeding her spoonfuls. She ate a big plate, and soon fell asleep sprawled across both their laps.

They talked quietly together so as not to disturb her. They both wished they could rewind the clock now and put their world of yesterday back together again. Soon the words dried up and for a while they both sat quietly looked at their daughter. She looked so perfect despite this awful thing inside her.

The night drifted on, television barely seen. They sat their side by side, both lost in their thoughts and barely speaking. Finally, roused by the midnight chime, Mathew said, "I keep thinking, I wonder if those chemicals they sprayed me with in Vietnam and which seem to have caused my shakes could have caused this too. I will kill all those American bastards if I find it is true."

Now Catherine felt really scared, there was a hard madness to his voice that scared her almost more than what was happening to her child. She wrapped her arms around his body which was now trembling and said. "Please Mathew, please; we have to be both strong for Amelie, let us not let ourselves think like that."

Mathew nodded to her, as if trying to agree, but there was no conviction in his manner.

Packing up to return Amelie at the hospital the next day was the hardest thing Catherine had ever done. They had arranged to come be back at the hospital at ten o'clock.

First they had called around to her Gran's place where the rest of her family were staying. They had a cup of tea and toast while they had talked about what was to happen. Amelie was only allowed a drink of fruit juice and grizzled about being hungry. The doctor had said only fluids this morning, really just water but apple juice was OK which she liked. It was because she would have to have a sedative for some of the procedures, such as the X-Rays and a thing called a spinal tap, where they would check to see if there were any cancer cells in her brain or nerves. They would also take samples from her bone marrow at the same time to look for the abnormal cells there.

When they left her, their brave little girl looking so trusting, they were told they should come back to the hospital to meet the specialist at four o'clock in the afternoon when the results of most of the tests would be in and they could decide on the treatment. If it all went as planned they could bring Amelie home for one more night and then the treatment would start tomorrow after which she would have to stay in the hospital for about three weeks.

The day went very slowly, they went back to the hotel and made arrangements for Ella to give them extra help there for a few days. Lizzie and Robbie had also undertaken to assist, Robbie had done many barman jobs in his former life and Lizzie was a whiz with keeping track of books and money and also pretty good at the cooking from her own restaurant, so that was a big help.

But it was very hard to distract themselves. Every minute seemed like an hour while they were waiting for their afternoon appointment to come. A bit after three in the afternoon they found themselves heading up to the hospital, it was only ten minutes walk from the hotel and they had nothing to bring but themselves. They decided they might as well be up there early, just in case they could get to see their daughter before the meeting. The nurse was very helpful and brought them into the room where Amelie was sitting playing on the floor with some blocks, next to a little boy who was perhaps four. Both were absorbed so they just sat and watched.

Finally about quarter to four the specialist came in, carrying sheets of papers with all the test results and big plastic films. He brought them into a little room next door where he took them through all the results, her white blood cell count was extraordinarily high, and the X-Rays showed lots of little lumps in her glands and maybe some in her lungs. It was hard to be sure if there were any cancers in her lungs or other places but at least everything was small. The good news was they had found no cancer cells in her spinal fluid.

So, to give her the best chance, the specialist wanted to start the cancer treatment tomorrow. It would be done at the Children's Hospital, at Camperdown, which was only ten minutes drive away.

So tonight they should take her home and give her a good dinner and put her to bed early. Tomorrow they would need to bring her to the hospital by eight in the morning, and she was to have absolutely nothing to eat or drink after she woke in the morning.

So they brought her home. Lizzie had cooked a meal for them all in the hotel restaurant, timed for six o'clock. Several of the staff and patrons asked if they could join them for a minute to give little gifts to Amelie to brighten her stay in hospital. So Amelie sat in her high chair in the middle of the table, surrounded by many small gifts and cards of well wishes and enjoyed being the centre of attention.

Tonight she was bright as a button and full of chatter and laughing. She ate all her food with gusto. It was hard to believe there could be anything wrong with their little girl. At half past seven they made their excuses and brought her up to bed, then read her a story together until she fell asleep. It all seemed too normal to believe.

In the morning they were up early, leaving by seven thirty to take Amelie to Camperdown. On arrival it seemed like the hospital machine had taken them over, before they knew it they had filled in a pile of forms and were being walked through endless corridors until they arrived at a room with four small beds, each for another child of a similar age. They stayed with Amelie while she was settled in and then it was time to leave.

Catherine had thought that saying goodbye yesterday was hard, but today it was excruciating, looking at the small and trusting face of their daughter as they walked away. She found herself sobbing and holding on to Mathew for support as she walked down the corridor.

Chapter 17 - Treatment

The next three weeks passed in a blur. During the first week Amelie received the anti- cancer drugs, a course of treatment called induction therapy where they gave doses of the two chemotherapy drugs in combination, which was hoped to kill the cancer cells which had been evident in large numbers in both her blood and bone marrow. The doctors called her cancer, Acute Lymphoblastic Leukemia or ALL for short and told them it occurred most commonly in children aged between two and three.

If this induction therapy went well and her blood count and bone marrow returned to normal over the next month, then they would give her one further dose of the treatment to mop up any surviving cancer cells, and provided the cancer cells did not come back after that the treatment would cease and they would just conduct regular checks to ensure it stayed that way.

Amelie tolerated this first course of chemotherapy surprisingly well though she was restless and grumbled a lot. Her hair did not even start to fall out and she continued to eat well except for a couple days after the treatment ended and she only lost a small amount of weight. The worst thing was she was bored by being confined to bed and wanted to get out and start doing things again so it was hard to keep her entertained and keep her as still as the hospital required.

However they all took turns at entertaining her, Lizzie and Gran Patsy told her stories and read her books. Catherine brought in paper for drawing and did pictures with her and Mathew got her to help him making little wooden toys and building houses out of blocks. As she got better it got even harder to contain her but everyone considered this was a good sign so it was a small price to pay.

After three weeks all the abnormal cells were gone from her blood and bone marrow and there was evidence of new healthy red and white blood cells being produced. The X-Rays were also all clear of any signs of the cancer in her lungs and the lumps were gone from around her neck and under her arms.

The doctors considered the treatment had gone as well as could possibly be expected and expressed their confidence in a favorable outcome from here. Catherine and Mathew, along with Lizzie and Patsy crossed their fingers and toes and hoped it was true.

They expected the repeat treatment to go equally well a month later, now it was only Mathew and Catherine caring for their child, as Lizzie, Robbie and family had returned to Broome so their own children could return to school. Gran helped out when needed but they felt they had their life under control and could mostly manage on their own.

However Amelie got much sicker this time, she had vomiting and diarrhea for several days and lost a lot of weight. Then two weeks later all her hair began to fall out in great lumps, and soon there were only a few straggly bits left.

Surprising, despite Amelie getting much sicker this time, she was a much better patient. She no longer grumbled about being confined to bed and would play happily by herself with just her dolls for hours without appearing to get bored. However after three weeks, except for a little round bald head, with a light fuzz of new hair and a thinner face and body, she appeared to be back to her normal self, eating ravenously, full of chatter and mischief.

Once she was home she spent endless hours driving her red car around the apartment and, on quiet mornings as they tidied the hotel, Mathew would carry the car downstairs so she could drive it over the smooth wooden floors of the hotels bars and corridors. They could follow her progress by the clatter of the wheels over the joints in the floorboards and her babbling happy voice.

After another month it was as if this sickness was just a distant memory; they had their Amelie back, her face was round again with a mischievous grin and she gave out a stream of endless chatter with the bar workers and patrons. She had also become incredibly loving, often cuddled between them in the night and saying her prayers. "God Bless Mummy, I love her the best, God Bless Daddy, I love him the best, God bless Gran Lizzie and Great Gran Patsy, God bless Ella, God bless Robbie who helped Daddy make my dolls house."

In those nights when they held her close then gently lifted her to her own bed so they could join their own bodies undisturbed, they had started to talk about having another baby, the idea of creating new life alongside that of their little girl seemed fitting now they had her back.

Chapter 18 - A Month Gone - Hope

It was now into April, the heat of the summer was easing. Business was booming again, better than ever. It had taken a bit of a hit for the first two months when they were spending half their lives at the Children's Hospital but in the last month it had caught up and it was now looking to be their best ever year.

Balmain had started to be discovered by a richer set, people who loved the old houses so close to the city, buying into the neighborhood, bringing their own young families and good incomes with them, often professional people who were making a business success of their lives, along with a more Bohemian artistic set. There were still lots of regular old timers, who brought their pension payments, but alongside them were the new sets of the upwardly mobile and artistic and they valued the good meals the hotel served along with the Sunday afternoon music.

Amelie now had an inch of hair starting to reshape her head away from an Elfin look to a little girl look again. Ella had managed to tie a red bow into some of the longer strands, telling her it matched her red car and made her look like a racing driver and this became her main outfit. In the morning, before the car was banished to the upstairs it could be heard, wheels rattling, pedals clanking, along with Amelie making engine noises as it flew along the hotel passages, warning pedestrians to step aside.

Each fortnight they would take her in to the hospital for a blood check and each month for a bone marrow check. They hated these reminders but Amelie accepted it all with good grace, at most giving a little whimper when they put the needles in. So far all was clear. Mathew and Catherine found they almost did not want to know the results; they dared to hope yet feared lest something would fracture this joy, it was easier to live each day at a time and not to think of a future, beyond the immediate events.

Easter came in April; it was a time to take joy in life. They went to the Royal Easter Show and spent the day walking amongst the animal stalls. Amelie stroked the rabbits and guinea pigs and watched the cows and horses with a little person's awe of other creatures so large. They watched the events in the main arena and the wood chopping, all shared ice creams and hot dogs and tried the rides which were suitable for a two year old, the merry go round and dodgem cars. Finally, in the mid afternoon, when the heat of the day was making them all tired, they came home and all fell asleep together on the big bed of their apartment.

The next day was Easter Sunday and together with Gran Patsy they went to the big church on the hilltop, where they were married, giving thanks for their lives together and the returned health of their daughter.

They refused to look over the horizon but were grateful and said prayers of thanks for the precious life they had.

Chapter 19 - Failure

The last week in April was the two month checkup, two months since the end of the second chemo treatment. Amelie was still in fine form but in the last week she had lost some of her sparkle. It was not something clear, but as if her buoyant ebullience had faded at little. Perhaps it was that after sickness and sudden wellness, life was back to a steady state again.

Yet, as Mathew and Catherine together brought her to the hospital, they felt an edge of anxiety. Perhaps it was always thus with such times of new knowledge which they had allowed themselves to forget over the last month. Still they found themselves holding each other's hand tighter and hugging the daughter a little more closely.

The day proceeded with the banal tedium of normality, nothing to report, lots of waiting but still nothing to report as all the samples were collected and tests run. It would be tomorrow before the results were in, and the doctors scheduled an appointment with Mathew and Catherine for two pm. By then everything would be available, blood count and smear, bone marrow results and X-Rays of key body areas. There was no need for Amelie to come back then and Gran Patsy had offered to mind her now that Lizzie had returned to the Broome.

Both Catherine and Mathew slept badly that night, Mathew's bad dreams returned and Catherine could not shake a prickling anxiety as they waited for this moment of truth. They were in the hospital and waiting twenty minutes before their appointment was due, but there was no sign of either the specialist pediatrician, Dr McPherson, or oncologist Dr Ryan, who together were now managing the case. Finally, five minutes after the due meeting time they saw both doctors hurry by together and go into the meeting room. They glimpsed Dr

Roberts waiting inside as well. A further ten minutes went by with still no call for them to come in.

Finally the oncologist opened the door and invited them in. One look at his face and Catherine knew that all was not well.

Suddenly she did not want to know, to end their idyll in the sun. She felt an overpowering urge to take Mathew's hand and walk out the door untold. It was as if a part of her had this impossible hope that if the story was not told then it could not come true, to pick up her daughter and pack up their car and drive over the horizon, perhaps to return to the desert where an aboriginal medicine man could try and cast out the evil spirit that lurked inside her daughter.

But despite this will to run away her feet were glued to the floor, heavy lead boots restrained her from fleeing, instead she felt her insides turn to jelly as Mathew stood and took her reluctant hand to come inside.

The three doctors were arranged in a semicircle and spread out on the desk in front of them were the sheets of paper and X-Ray films which together constituted her daughter's future, a life writ in numbers and pictures on plastic.

Catherine forced her panicked brain to quieten its inner noise. She realized that one of the doctors had begun speaking, though it had not penetrated. She made her mind listen.

She replayed the last two sentences stored in her memory bank.

"I wish we could tell you that all is fine and there are no signs that the cancer has returned. Unfortunately that is not the case."

Mathew spoke, "What are you saying, Doctor?"

"I am afraid we can see cells that look like cancer cells, abnormal lymphocytes with rapid division, in your daughter's bone marrow. They should not be there. And there are also some suspicious shadows on the chest X-Rays that look like tumors are beginning to regrow in her lungs."

Mathew turned to the doctors and said, "I have been reading that Vietnam Veterans' children have an increased risk of cancer. What do you know about that?"

Mathew continued, "They say it is from dioxin which contaminated the Agent Orange they sprayed us all with and which damages our DNA, increasing the risk of cancers in ourselves but also damage can be passed on to our children and cause cancer in them. Could this be the cause of what has happened to my daughter, that she got the cancer from me?

The oncologist shook his head, "I don't know and can't say for sure, but it seems unlikely. However I have not read up in this area, so others would be better qualified to answer than I am. But when these things happen there is no point trying to find something or someone to blame. That helps no one. It is not your daughter's fault, it is not your wife's fault, it is not your fault. The best thing you can do is focus on your daughter and stay positive. That is what works best."

Mathew replied, with something like an angry growl resonating through his voice. "I am not blaming my daughter, I am not blaming my wife, I am not really blaming myself though some of my mates told me it was best not to get married and have children.

"I am blaming the government of Australia who sent us there without protection and most of all I blame those American bastards who dropped spray all over the country to poison the trees. They did not give a damn if they poisoned all the people and animals who lived there as well."

Catherine felt herself cringe inside at her husband's anger. Her whole world of false hopes was collapsing around her; she wanted him to help her and Amelie. She did not want him to not fight with and blame the world. Perhaps he was right in some way but what point was there to it all, as the doctor said the priority needed to be to help Amelie get better.

She took Mathew's hand, "Please can we go home now, tomorrow we can talk to the doctors about what to do. I just want to hold my little girl and feel your arms around me too."

Something in the desperation of her voice must have got through to him; he stood up and brought her home, his arm around her shoulders. That night the three of them slept together, wrapped in a joint embrace. It was as if by holding each other they could hold away the next day.

Chapter 20 - Fading Hope

In the morning Catherine rang and told her mother of the test results, trying to keep the devastation out of her voice. It was hard to tell her Gran last night, saying it again to her mother was like a double body blow.

She finished by saying, "Mum, I am so scared, and Mathew is taking it really bad as well, he is blaming himself from being sprayed with chemicals in Vietnam, saying he had given this to Amelie. He is so angry."

Lizzie cut through this at once. "Oh my, Cathy, I am so sorry. I will book the first flight I can to Sydney to come and help you. Robbie can mind the business here and the other children. Together we will all find a way through this."

That day she and Mathew discussed what to do, both together and with the doctors. Mathew was opposed to further treatment. He kept saying that putting yet another poison into Amelie, trying to kill the cancer cells with yet more poison, when it was first caused by a poison, was crazy. He said he wanted nothing further to do with it, this chemotherapy thing, he knew it would only make Amelie really sick again like last time.

However he had no other solution about what could be done and he agreed that the cancer could not just be allowed to spread through her body unchecked. So together they talked to their doctors and then got second opinions from other specialists.

At last Mathew agreed to a treatment plan which involved using radiation, which had not been used before, along with a moderate dose of chemotherapy that might in combination give a fair chance of controlling the cancer on the second go.

They knew the odds of success were now below 50%. But by the end of all the talk they had both agreed that they could not just abandon all hope for their daughter to this disease. However, even when the decision was made, Mathew said he still hated what they were subjecting Amelie to. Catherine could not disagree with him, but she refused to give up hope that this time it would work fully and cure her.

By the time they had reached agreement Lizzie had arrived. She tried to give them support in their decision saying it was an awful choice but if it had been up to her she would have done the same thing too.

When the day came to take Amelie back to hospital and start the new round of treatment, Mathew asked Lizzie and Cathy to take her, he was morose and clearly did not want to have to face yet another round of medical meetings and waiting. He hugged Amelie tightly and promised to come and see her the next day.

The treatment ran over another two weeks then there was a two week period for Amelie to recover before they retested her to see how it had worked. Amelie was really sick over the second and third weeks, she lost a lot of weight, she was five pounds lighter than when it started, her hair was all gone again and her face and arms were pitifully thin.

In the fourth week she started to eat properly again and put some weight back, but now she had developed a persistent low grade cough, and sure enough when the time came the X-Rays showed that the lumps in her lungs had not fully gone away and she also had a low grade pneumonia that required ongoing treatment with antibiotics before it started to settle down.

But she was a wonderful patient, so sweet and uncomplaining, with barely a whimper when they gave her needles and always happy to see the nurses and doctors and with cheerful things to say to other patients.

Sometimes Catherine desperately wanted her cross and crotchety daughter back, wishing for more fight in her soul to rage against this disease that was consuming her body. But she and everyone else had also fallen in love with delightful little girl who suffered it all so bravely.

At first Mathew came to the hospital every day to visit her, but after a week as she got sicker he started missing visits, it was obviously tearing him up inside each time he saw her decline. So he started to make excuses and take refuge in not coming, instead giving the others presents to bring to her, drawings and little toys he made.

Amelie seemed not to mind, she accepted all his gifts with joy. Each time there came to visit she asked Cathy and Lizzie to give him a hug and kiss specially from her.

Finally at the end of the third week Amelie was well enough to return home and for a short time their life returned to something like normality.

They all knew that Amelie was not better, the cancer cells were still growing away in her bone marrow and the tumors remained in her lungs.

But for almost a month she seemed to have improved. The doctors gave instructions to feed her up, give her lots of attention and try and get her as strong as could be before considering new treatment options.

Chapter 21 - Madness

As if she did not have enough to worry about with Amelie, Catherine had a new worry. Mathew had begun to have lots of bad dreams again. She remembered they had begun around the time she had the miscarriage in the second half of last year; but with so much else since it was hard to remember exactly when.

Her memory was that since then they had ebbed and flowed, at times stopping for a week or two and then returning for two or three nights. But since Amelie had got sick they had occurred more and more. Now they were happening more nights than not. She found, in her own exhausted state, both emotional and physical, it was harder to give Mathew the level of attention she thought he needed.

Now, more and more, she found herself resenting this additional disruption to her life. On some nights when she woke up to his tossing and turning she had started to go out to the lounge room, closing the door to the bedroom to cut off the noise of his muttering and the disturbance of his restless sleep.

As she looked at him in this place she could feel anger bubbling up inside her at what seemed like his self-indulgence but alongside that sat a love for this man and distress for his torment. But overall her dominant feeling was an almost total exhaustion of body and spirit.

Sometimes she curled up and fell asleep again on the lounge, other times she lay on the floor in Amelie' room. She no longer slept in the bed with Amelie as she did not want to disturb her much needed sleep with her own restlessness.

The few times she had laid in with her, Amelie had woken her saying, "Mummy, are you having bad dreams? You are moving so much. I don't want to worry."

She loved her daughter's sweet face as she said it and her evident concern, but it was unfair to Amelie, she need her sleep to build her own strength much more. But if she felt Amelie stirring she would sit beside her on the bed, cuddle and stroke her to try and give her comfort in whatever way she could.

She knew the outlook for Amelie was becoming more and more desperate. Next week she was booked in for one more round of chemo, and this would be the last one, it was making her so sick it was just no point in keeping going, as the last time the tumours had barely gone away before they started growing again.

There was no sign of them yet outside, under her arms and neck and in her mouth, but there were still ones inside her that had not really shrunk much after the last treatment.

They had agreed they would try one more time, to try and shrink them a bit more and then they would try a thing called immunotherapy to try and boost Amelie's own immunity to fight off the disease.

Catherine wondered if they should go straight to the immunotherapy thing now, the idea of submitting her poor brave little girl to this awful chemo even one more time seemed both horrible and pointless.

Yet, not to try seemed to be an admission of defeat, and somehow they had to keep their own hope alive, but then they could not let their own desire for hope cause Amelie unnecessary and pointless suffering.

She tried not to let the "dying" word into her mind. But somewhere in a deep recess of her mind it was there anyway and she knew they may all have to face up to it soon, that everything modern medicine had to offer seemed unable to save the life of their little girl. But for now, each time the thought tried to rise in her mind, she pushed it firmly back into its buried cave, determined to keep it locked in there.

Mathew had become increasingly unreliable in the business. She had stopped rostering him on his own, as on these days that meant it often fell to her, as he just would not come out and serve people until they go really impatient. She did not want to lose custom as she needed to try and keep the business functioning to pay all the bills.

Instead he would sit out the back reading. He seemed to have an endless stream of books and magazines he was reading, often medical ones. She had welcomed it at first, something to occupy his mind and give him purpose, reading all the latest research on cancer treatments, all the pros and cons of the different options.

But as it began to occupy ever more of his time she started to wonder what he was really looking for. She felt she understood all the medical options; the problem was they just were not working.

So she started to pay more attention to what he was reading, wondering why. She noticed an ever increasing focus on the effects of chemicals, sprays like Agent Orange, their effects on exposed people, their long term effects, the potential to cause harm to one's own children.

He was starting to talk more and more about how he had been poisoned by these bastards and now the poison was spreading to his little girl. He would say, "I am sick and she is even sicker and it's all their fault."

At other times he would talk repeatedly about how it was his own fault that Amelie had got sick, he had been warned by other Vets that he should not have children. He had ignored these warnings and now his little girl was paying for it.

Catherine tried to discuss this rationally with him. She did not know if it was true that there were these sorts of effects, the medical opinion seemed divided. But, even if there were, it was pointless to try and blame himself or someone else, they just had to stick together and try and support their little girl and help her get better.

She would say, "It's no help to blame anyone, we just need to focus on Amelie and give her all the love we can."

But Mathew seemed to have stopped listening to her, each day it seemed that his mind wandered further and further into this maze of blame and recriminations. Catherine was sure it was also part of the problem with all his bad dreams, that he was dreaming these things and sleeping badly as they endlessly went around in his mind.

Each new day he would wake up, exhausted in mind and body, and then spending further hours feeding his imagination in reading new things of this type before dreaming them all over again in an ever increasing and crazy spiral of despair.

She wished she knew how she could help him. If Amelie was not so sick and managing the hotel without him was not so hard, perhaps she could have found some way to connect with him. But now she was so chronically exhausted herself that her patience with what seemed like his self-indulgent escapism was fading. More and more she was starting to snap at him.

Yesterday she had said. "For God sake put those crazy magazines and books away. Come and help me at the bar."

He had done it reluctantly for an hour, but then, after the bar closed, he had stayed up until almost three o'clock in the morning reading this crazy stuff and, almost as soon as he had come to bed he had woken her with another of his dreams, mumbling, "I am going to kill them. I will buy a gun and go and kill those murdering and poisoning bastards."

It was awful and it gave her shivers but at least he was asleep when he said it, if he said something like that in real life she did not know what she would do."

The next morning Amelie's breathing was quite strained and her gums were pasty. Catherine had a sinking feeling as she arranged to bring her into the doctor for more tests.

It was breaking her heart, her little girl was so brave, and she was smiling brightly and telling her Mum not to worry, but it was so obvious she clearly was not alright.

Catherine had tried to talk to Amelie a few times about what was happening but it was very hard, it was as if she both understood and chose not to know.

It seemed that Amelie now just lived in the moment, most often sitting in her favourite red car with her favourite doll sitting on the seat alongside her. Once there would have been too little space for her and the doll together but now she had grown so thin that the doll fitted easily alongside her.

As she got ready Mathew was still sleeping, after staying awake most of the night. She knew he would not want to come to hospital and face up to the actuality of what was needed. So she decided, when she left to go to the hospital, to leave him sleeping away, he may be more rational with more sleep. She wrote him a short note, telling him where they had gone and left in a taxi.

Once at the hospital she waited for what seemed a long time until the doctor had examined Amelie before deciding what to do next. He decided they should take fresh blood samples to check her white and red cell levels, to see whether she had become anaemic and also whether her white cells had bounced back up and how many were healthy versus abnormal cancerous ones. He also wanted to look at the size of the tumours in her chest. Once they had this information they could decide on what further treatment options they should pursue.

After three hours of queuing and waiting they finally had all the procedures done and the chest X-Rays developed. Amelie was sitting playing with some blocks on the floor of the waiting room when the radiologist and doctor called to her to come in and view the results.

She asked the receptionist if she would keep an eye on her girl while she went into the consulting room, leaving the door open. The radiologist pointed to the current chest X-Ray and the one taken a fortnight before. It was clear from first glance that the black spaces in her lungs were getting smaller and the white lumps were getting bigger.

While Catherine knew deep down that this was happening she felt her heart fall through the floor as this clear sign of the cancer starting to overwhelm her daughter. She could feel the tears forming in her eyes and tried to brush them away with the back of her hand.

The doctor started to discuss the findings, saying, "The blood count is very low, her red cells are barely responding. Even though her white cells have not gone up there are more cancer cells and less normal cells than before.

I think we need to give her a whole blood transfusion, part of her breathlessness is probably from the anaemia as well as the tumours, so she may benefit from some oxygen as well. I think we should hospitalise her for the day while we do that and once we have got her red blood count back to normal we can see how she is.

Perhaps you need to ask her husband to come in so that we can all discuss further treatment options from here.

Catherine found herself unable to listen, she could not help crying and pushed a handkerchief into her mouth to stifle the sobs, it felt hopeless.

The doctor put his hand on her shoulder in a fatherly fashion, saying, "Why don't you ring your husband and get him to come in? Then we can all sit down and discuss where to go from here.

"In the meantime Amelie can stay in the hospital and we will start her on oxygen and a blood transfusion."

Catherine nodded and the receptionist gave her the phone to use. She rang her home, there was no answer, she rang instead to the bar and Ella answered, she had just come in and was surprised to find there was no sign of Mathew though she had yet to go upstairs and check on him.

Catherine asked her to call him to come to the phone, in case he was upstairs and had been unable to get to the phone a minute ago.

Ella returned saying, "There is no sign of him but there is something really worrying, there is a gun case for a revolver on the table but without the gun, and there is a note with your name written on it, inside a sealed envelope on the table. I have not opened it but perhaps you should come home and have a look.

Cathy rang Lizzie who was staying with her Gran and asked her to come into the hospital to mind Amelie while she went home. Then she talked to her Gran and asked her to come up to the hotel. Of all the people who knew Mathew she seemed to be the one he listened to best, perhaps because she had known him since he was a boy.

Lizzie said she would be in the hospital as soon as a taxi could get her there so Catherine told Amelie she had to go home and get her Daddy and in the meantime she should go with the nurse who would put her in a bed and give her a funny mask to put on her face, and that her own Grandma Lizzie would be in with her soon.

As always Amelie just took it in her stride, giving a bright smile and a hug and kiss and finishing with, "Love you Mummy."

Then Catherine walked outside and caught another taxi home. Her Gran was just arriving as she did and they went upstairs together, after talking briefly to Ella who said she had seen no sign still of Mathew, but his car which was normally parked in the back lane was gone.

Upstairs the scene was just as Ella had described it. She could see that Mathew had showered and put on clean clothes, though there was no sign he had eaten any breakfast.

She opened the note. It read.

Dear Catherine,

I have decided to go and fix those people who poisoned me and now Amelie. It is all the fault of the chemicals they sprayed me with that made me sick and are now making my little girl sick.

Even now they are still poisoning her with that chemical therapy and radiation they are giving her, and all of it is making her sicker and sicker.

So I have to find some medicine that does not make Amelie sick and will make her better.

I know our defence people who work at Victoria Barracks have good medicines that can be used to treat the poisons; they give them to soldiers who work for them to protect them. They could use these to make Amelie better but they are keeping them hidden away, to make sure the rest of the world does not know.

I am going there to get them to give me the medicines. I may have to shoot one or two of them to get them to listen to me and help me but I am happy to do whatever it takes.

Someone has to stand up to them and make them do the right thing. So I have taken on this job.

Your ever loving husband

Mathew

Catherine felt terror grip her. She swayed and had to grab the edge of the table to hold herself upright as her thoughts churned. *What if he tries to shoot someone, then the police or military would shoot him instead. Then he would be dead. That was no way to help her daughter.*

Mathew was the one thing apart from Amelie that remained really precious in her life. Sure he had gone a bit crazy with the pain, but she believed she could help fix that when there was time.

Patsy, standing next to her, reached out to steady her, looking at her with concern, her own face tense.

Catherine passed her the note, watching her Gran's face intently as comprehension dawned.

"Oh my God," was all her Gran said.

Then she came and put her arms around Catherine, saying, "You poor darling. He is a good man, but now, with all the grief and anger of what has happened, something inside his mind has gone wrong. We must call the police and ask them to look for him before he hurts someone else or gets hurt himself."

Catherine could not stand it anymore; she sat on a chair, holding the note, her whole body shaking with sobs. It was all too terrible for words; she could not bear to lose Mathew too.

She watched her Gran pick up the phone and dial the police, In five minutes two constables were there with her, reading the note and looking around at the evidence. Her Grandmother briefly explained what had happened to Amelie, her sickness, and then of Mathew's mental state, imploring them to be careful, both for their own safety and for his too.

Then the police were on the phone calling for backup and giving the base details to get officers to the Victoria Barracks front gate, and also to ring the Barracks to give a warning.

As these arrangements were being made Catherine sat, only half listening and unmoving. As they were leaving, they said to her, she was to wait here for now.

It brought her to life; an image came unbidden to her mind of a crazed Mathew walking towards a police man and a soldier pointing a gun. Then the policeman shooting Mathew dead, claiming it was self-defence.

She knew she must try to stop this, she grabbed at the policeman's arm, saying, "I have to come, I have to see him and make him stop."

The policeman went to brush her off and pushed past her to leave, walking towards the front door.

Now her Grandmother, who was standing closest to the door, put her own body in the way, blocking the door, forceful but measured.

"Officer, my granddaughter is right; we have to come there too. Mathew knows us and will trust us whereas he will just see you as a threat. We have to try and stop one tragedy becoming an even bigger tragedy. My granddaughter's own daughter is gravely ill of cancer. This man, Mathew, is the little girl's father. He is a good man but driven mad with grief. It will help no one if he gets shot in the process. We have a much better chance of stopping him if we are both there to try and talk and reason with him, to get him to give up his gun and go and have treatment for the illness which has taken over his own mind.

"Many years ago I failed to act when I should have and my own husband died of my stupidity. I will not let it happen a second time with my granddaughter's husband.

"So officer, I insist you bring both me and Catherine with you and give us the chance to talk to Mathew first before anyone else does something foolhardy. If you try to stop us coming with you any consequences will be on your head."

Reluctantly the officer gave way and motioned for them both to come with him.

In a minute they were racing across the city towards Paddington, sirens blaring. The police car pulled to a stop in Oxford Street in front of Victoria Barracks. There were six other policemen and the same number of soldiers in position, all armed and guarding the gates. There was no sign of Mathew.

They piled out of the car and the police ran over to join their fellow officers.

Catherine looked around wildly. She glimpsed Mathew, across the road and hiding unobtrusively in a shop entrance, something in his hand tucked out of sight.

She ran across the street, heedless of the screeching and honking traffic, determined to shield Mathew with her body. That way they would shoot her before they shot him. Then she was in front of him.

He had a mad look in his eyes and the gun was in his hand. He looked up at her, saying, "Catherine, what are you doing here, you need to get out of the way and let me do what I need to do, I have to make them give me the medicine."

She looked over her shoulder, several police men were following close behind with their guns drawn and trained on them both. She pushed her body towards Mathew, determined to keep her body between him and them. He tried to step to one side, she moved with him.

Suddenly a clear voice spoke out from behind her, it was her Gran. "Mathew."

He looked up, temporarily frozen. Her Gran stepped up around Catherine until she was standing directly in front of Mathew, the pistol pointing at her own belly.

Wordlessly she reached out and took the pistol by the barrel, turned it to the side and removed it from his hands. She passed the gun back to Catherine.

She wrapped her arms around Mathew, saying, "My boy, my poor boy, this won't help anyone. We must find another way to help Amelie. I need you to help me do that by first putting this silly thing away, then helping me look for something that really will cure her."

Something in her words and tone got through to him when nothing else had; he nodded and the mad gleam slowly faded from his eyes.

The police came over and put handcuffs around his wrists, then led him to the back of the police van. Catherine was pleased he was being treated gently, almost kindly by the officers who had taken him away.

She realised she had not moved, frozen in place, with the gun still in her own hands. She wanted to move to run after him and hug him, to say it would be alright.

But another part of her was shaking with rage and she found herself unable to move. *How could he have been so stupid? Yes he was upset, but this was beyond crazy. But for the quick thinking of Gran he could be lying dead on the pavement now.* It made her so mad that he could allow his life to be wasted like that for no point, part of her wanted to hug him but another part of her wanted to hit him for his stupidity.

So instead of going to him she just stood there, rooted to the spot, her own mind frozen.

Mathew climbed inside the back of the police van, trying to look back at her. She could have sworn he was trying to say sorry, but she refused to meet his eyes.

Then he was gone and they locked the door. The senior officer came over to talk to both Catherine and her grandmother, saying "We will hold him in a cell in the local police station and arrange for a psychiatrist to assess him as soon as possible and work out what to do.

"He may have to be hospitalised in Callan Park for the time being to make sure he is not at risk of harming himself or others."

Catherine nodded. Then, realising she was still holding the gun, she passed it to the police officer.

The following morning a judge gave orders, that following the preliminary examination, Mathew was to be held in Beveridge House in Callan Park, a high security facility for the insane. There he was to undergo further evaluation, for an indefinite period until they determined what treatment was required.

Catherine had stood in the back of the court, unable to speak and still unable to meet Mathew's eyes, she could find no words to say to either help or harm him, it was like his confinement and madness had frozen over a part of her soul.

It was left to her Grandmother Patsy and her own Mum to try and explain the circumstances and the need for compassion. All that day Catherine sat in a chair barely moving, leaving it to Lizzie to visit and care for Amelie and for her Gran to manage the hotel. She ate the food that was put in front of her mechanically, she did not cry, she just sat and stared and wondered where her life had gone.

Finally in the evening Lizzie came to her and made her stand up, shower and go to bed, saying. "It is time for you to return to see your daughter."

The following day, when Catherine came to hospital to visit her, Amelie did not ask where her Daddy was. Instead she asked that her red car and also the house for it that her Daddy had made be brought into the hospital and put alongside her bed. It was as if she knew her father could not come and somehow the thing he had made for her birthday would have to take his place.

To Catherine this was even more heart wrenching, as if Amelie knew that this hospital room had become a final bedroom and, if she could not have her father, at least she would have something in this room that reminded her of him.

The doll's house, with the car inside took up a big space in the room. A couple of the nurses and doctors grumbled that it was in the way, but in the end they understood that, if it made this little girl happy, that was a small price to pay.

Chapter 22 - Last Chance – A Transplant

Patsy and Lizzie had discussed between themselves how best to support Catherine and Amelie over this time and had agreed that one of them needed to focus on going to see Mathew every day and also putting time in at the hotel, to at least keep it turning over enough money to pay the family's bills, and the other needed to focus on supporting Catherine and Amelie.

As Patsy knew the people of Balmain from more than four decades of living there and also had known Mathew since he was a boy she took on this part, she had spent an hour with Ella working out the roster yesterday, she had also taken it upon herself to directly manage the restaurant and catering side, though she would draw on Lizzie's knowledge here. She would also do back up bar work as required.

In addition Patsy had set aside two hours each day just after lunch to go and spend with Mathew, to get him to tell her about all his ideas, even his most crazy ones, until she understood both his concerns and whether he had ideas that could be useful. She would also pass on the news from Amelie and Catherine back to him.

Catherine appeared to be too angry with him to talk directly to him at this stage even though Patsy knew it would pass.

Yesterday Patsy had spent over two hours talking to Mathew, telling him about Catherine and how upset she had been, telling him about Amelie and what the options there were and asking his opinion.

She had also asked him to tell her about all the things he had been reading. She found him surprisingly lucid about these, though wracked by guilt about his own contribution. He told of studies which showed the effects of the chemical agents which had been sprayed in Vietnam and how he had been repeatedly drenched in them, the direct effects of the chemicals and a particular contaminant called dioxin which had definitely contaminated batches of Agent Orange he had been exposed to. He explained how there was now increasing evidence that dioxin could damage a person's DNA and be passed on to the children that way.

So Mathew was sure that defects in Amelie's bone marrow had been passed to her from him as a result of these poisonous chemicals and now they had to find a way to repair her DNA. He had read about research being done by the US and Australian Military to investigate treatments for these things. He told Patsy how, even though it was top secret, he knew they had found things which could work and how he needed to find out more about these and get them to treat his daughter.

He even told her of a technique he had read about where the cells of a healthy donor, which matched the sick person, could be injected into that person; it was called a bone marrow transplant. They were just starting to try it, mainly overseas, but also in some Australian hospitals. While Patsy did not understand the complex science she could see that this idea had logic to it. She promised she would pass it on to Cathy to tell to the doctors.

That night she reported back on all Mathew had said, saying she wanted Lizzie and Cathy to ask the doctors about whether it was an option to try a bone marrow transplant.

Two days after Catherine watched the judge order her husband into confinement in a mental hospital Catherine found herself at a meeting with the doctors to discuss the remaining treatment options for Amelie. Now that Mathew could no longer participate she asked her mother to come with her, while Patsy stayed at the hotel.

The doctors explained that they had stabilized Amelie's condition with the blood transfusion which had brought her red cell count back up to the normal range. They were now of the opinion that they should try one more lot of chemotherapy to see if they could get the tumors to shrink again, as they were starting to run out of other choices.

After trying this final round of chemotherapy the only treatment options that remained were things that were only really experimental. These included immunotherapy and some new chemotherapy agents. So they suggested they make a final treatment attempt using a really high dose of chemotherapy, along with immunotherapy as a last ditch attempt to stop the cancer or at least slow it down greatly.

Since Mathew's outburst Catherine found herself asking more questions in her mind rather than just accepting that the doctors knew best in all things. Not that these medical people were arrogant or unwilling to listen, it was just that all that they had tried was failing and they seemed to have run out of ideas.

So now it seemed to Catherine that all they had to offer was more of the same chemotherapy at even higher doses, combined with some new immunotherapy agents to help Amelie's body recover.

As she questioned the oncologist explained that the purpose of the immunotherapy was to boost the production of Amelie's own immune cells and also help the chemotherapy drugs to kill the damaged cancer cells. That way they hoped she would recover from the chemotherapy faster and the treatment would also aid the process of removing the damaged cancer cells and also getting her own bone marrow back to working properly in producing new red cells to carry oxygen and white cells to fight other diseases.

They explained that part of the problem was that the treatment was continually damaging Amelie's own immunity to common infections and so they now had to start to be really careful that she did not catch some common disease which, in a healthy person, would be harmless.

Now her mother, Lizzie, ever curious, starting adding more questions to challenge to doctors and search for new ideas. Catherine could see the doctors were becoming uncomfortable as the questions continued, but this was far too important to give up so she and Lizzie kept burrowing in to what they were saying.

When it was clear the doctors had no more answers to give Catherine said, "So are you saying that because of the treatment she has already had, along with the extra you want to give her, that something like a common cold could make her really sick and even kill her."

The oncologist replied, "That is often what happens with long term cancer patients, that it is not the cancer that kills them but an infection like a pneumonia which we could otherwise control. Some people even consider it a blessing when that happens as, by leading to death, it spares the person continued suffering."

Catherine felt her mind reeling, even though she had always known that death was a possibility, their language had now changed to talking about it as if it was inevitable.

Lizzie burrowed in again, "So are you saying that if we give her more chemotherapy and particularly at an even higher dose we make it more likely that Amelie will die from some other infection."

The doctor looked a bit startled at this logical leap, "Yes, I suppose you could say that."

Catherine continued on, "So what is the point of further treatment, more chemotherapy, if it only damages her immunity further, what is the chance that it can still cure her?

The doctor replied, "It is now less than ten percent I would think. There was originally around a three quarters chance that we would get long term remission, but I am afraid that has now become very unlikely."

Catherine continued, "So, why are you proposing that we give her more of the same treatment? Last time it made her really sick. As well as all her hair falling out she had severe vomiting and diarrhea for days and lost lots of weight, not to mention that she felt really unwell and miserable for almost two weeks.

"Is that all you are offering us? That she gets more of that only this time it will be even worse and yet, despite the amount she suffers from the treatment, she will almost certainly die anyway. If so why are you proposing it?"

The doctor replied, "We are just trying to slow the cancer down and buy her more time, maybe a few more months of life if it works really well. It would be foolish to hope for more.

"You have to start preparing for the fact that your daughter will be unlikely to make another Christmas, no matter what we do. You should prepare yourself, your husband and Amelie for this."

Catherine felt crushed, she sat in the chair with her face in her hands; she did not want to hear or think about this. She supposed she must.

She started to feel more and more of what Mathew was going through; rage against life's unfairness, except that in his case he blamed himself too.

As she thought of him she remembered that he had told Patsy, her Grandmother, something that he wanted them to ask the doctors about. She must try and remember what it was that Patsy had said he was talking about, the thing her wanted her to ask the doctor about, something about a transplant.

Lizzie was not willing to leave the conversation at that. "Doctor, you talked about various experimental treatments, new drugs, this thing called immunotherapy, perhaps other things. Could you please tell us all you know about these things?"

Catherine could see the oncologist now felt he was on safer ground. He started to go through and describe the other options in more detail. None of them sounded of much value to her, little more than vain hopes, unlikely to give a cure and just involve more unpleasant treatments.

Her mind was half inside her head and half listening until the words, "Bone Marrow Transplant", were said. That was what Patsy said Mathew had been talking about.

She turned and looked directly at the doctor, "Please tell me about this bone marrow transplant."

The doctor replied, "Well it is still a relatively experimental treatment. It is high risk, because it involves using high doses of the chemotherapy agents along with radiation, to kill all the remaining bone marrow and cancer cells in the body. Then, in a few days, when all these cells in the bone marrow have died along with the cancer cells, new healthy cells are given to the person. Provided the body does not reject them and they start growing inside the person's own bone marrow they can replace the person's own cells that were there before the treatment killed them.

"So, if we can kill all the bad cancer cells and then get the new cells not to be rejected, the result is that, after that time, the patient has these new stem cells in their bone marrow. They are no longer their own cells but ones that have come from the other person. They grow and reproduce forming a new, healthy population of red and white cells with no cancer.

"However, the downside is that if the cells do not take then we have killed off all the remaining bone marrow cells in the person's own body. If that happens then, within a few weeks at most, the person will die. That is because they can no longer produce the red cells in their blood which carry the oxygen, or the white cells which give them immunity or the platelets which allow their blood to clot.

"We have already thought about this option, not that we have tried it before in this hospital. But in the last few days we have been researching all other choices. However we have one big problem. In order for the new cells to be compatible and start growing in your daughter's body they have to match her own cells in some important ways;, this matching is what we call histocompatibility. It means that the surface of these cells have to appear the same as the surface of the cells in Amelie's own body or else her own body will reject them as foreign and kill them before they can establish.

"So we have done some preliminary screening on what we call the histocompatibility profile of your daughter, a thing called the Major Histocompatibility Complex.

"Your daughter has a very unusual version, something that is rarely seen in Anglo-Saxon Australians, it is more found in Pacific Islanders and New Guineans, but then she also has some European factors that are not normally found in these islander people. So, as a result, we have checked all the registered donors to see if we have a match. So far we have been unable to find anyone who appears suitable. Those few who we have found who could be donors with the typical Pacific Islanders complex, have the wrong factors for the Amelie's Anglo-Saxon heritage.

"So, while we could try a less than perfect donor, we would have to use very high doses of anti-rejection drugs to have any chance and, even then, it is still likely to fail. If that happened all that would result is to kill your daughter even faster in trying this bone marrow transplant.

"We will of course keep looking and, should we find a suitable donor, we will let you know. We would also encourage you to have yourselves tested along with all your friends and relations in the event that some of them have the right histocompatibility complex factors.

"But at this stage I would not like you raise your hopes about this only to have them dashed yet again. That is why I have not discussed it so far."

Catherine nodded to the assembled group, "Well, if that is all that is left to us, then that is what we must try. I do not want my daughter to have any more chemotherapy unless there is a real chance of it curing her, it is unfair on her to put her through it unless it has is a long term purpose.

"However as soon as possible I would like you to test me and see if I am a suitable donor. I am sure her father will also want to be tested as soon as possible. I will also ask all my other family and friends to do the same. So we must hope that one of us has the correct combination.

"Could you also keep looking in other places for suitable donors, perhaps in places like New Zealand, Fiji or Hawaii, in such people the right combination of factors may be more common."

The doctors nodded and it was agreed.

Chapter 23 - Donor Required

Two weeks went by while Catherine arranged for all her friends to be tested, Lizzie did the same with all her extended family, her mother, the other children, even Robbie though unrelated, and her great uncle and his children who lived in Melbourne. There were good matches to some people except for the one critical genetic component, what the doctors called the Melanesian associated genes.

The doctors checked transplant registers in other Australian cities and New Zealand but no matches were found there either, and it was not considered feasible to look further afield as the ability to get a donor to Sydney, even if one was found, was too hard. The chance of finding a donor with the right genotype outside the western Pacific seemed remote.

At the same time Catherine and Lizzie had taken to investigating everything they could find out about bone marrow transplants and tissue matching. The results were variable but when the match was good then the results were surprisingly good, up to 80% success, whereas it was disastrous to do a transplant with a poor match. They knew they could not subject Amelie to a transplant unless the match was good.

They had both become walking encyclopedias about the science of histocompatibility. They understood that this thing was referred to in the text books as HLA typing and measured things called antigens on the surface of the white cells, and that these fell in groups based on four closely linked genes on what was called Chromosome 6, a particular one of the 23 human chromosomes which made up a person's DNA.

They had found plenty of people who could match Amelie for her first three genes, including Catherine's own adopted father; it was the fourth one that eluded them in the right combination with the others.

The knowledge did not help Amelie but at least it gave her and Lizzie a common purpose and something to do in the many hours they shared, both while sitting and talking with Amelie and amongst themselves. At night they would sit up at home for hours with Patsy and they would tell her news of Amelie and their day and she would tell them about Mathew.

Catherine knew she must go and see her husband but she still could not bring herself to. On the one hand she felt anger towards him for what he had done; the putting of himself in harm's way for no purpose. But in another way she felt a strange sort of admiration for his courage to risk anything to save his daughter. She also knew there was nothing he could do for his daughter right now. Therefore she procrastinated about going to visit him and trying to arrange for him to be able to visit Amelie.

She knew, from her Grandma, that he was mostly calm. But he also had occasional periods of manic craziness, when he still made threats. These had been reduced by medicine he was on, though he did not like it because he said it made him dopey.

Grandma was also talking to the doctors who examined him and they were become less concerned about his mental state now and discussing the option of allowing him out on day release provided he had taken his medication before he left.

Catherine was not so sure; she could not bear a repeat of what had happened before. She had this uncontrollable terror that his madness would return and it would end up worse.

She felt unable to cope with that along with dealing with the issues about Amelie and, even if it was not really fair to keep him locked up, part of her just felt relief that he was safe and out of harm's way.

Amelie was not doing well but rarely complained. She was constantly breathless, her lips had a faint blue tinge, her weight kept steadily falling away. She bravely tried to eat the food they offered, because she knew it pleased them, but now even eating seemed to exhaust her.

Her greatest delight seemed to be the car and its house, she would spend hours just looking her red car, and often asked to be lifted down to sit in it as she could no longer climb in and out of bed on her own. But, after a few minutes of sitting up in it, she would ask to be lifted back up to bed, even sitting up seemed to tire her now.

It was funny how Lizzie and Catherine had started not to notice her daily deterioration and her ever decreasing ability to do things. It was as if it was so gradual that it passed them by, though their minds understood and they were gripped by an urgency to find a donor.

Amelie' inexorable slide was only brought home to them one day when Patsy visited with them. She had not been in for four days with the work at the hotel, visiting Mathew and talking to his doctors.

But that day, when she came in she said, out loud, on seeing Amelie, "My poor pet, you are wasting away before my eyes and your lips are getting bluer and your breath is getting shorter.

Amelie just nodded at her, then said, "Grandma it is true, I am getter sicker each day aren't I, but I am trying to be brave and Sophie helps me, she talks to me inside my head and says she will help me be brave, so it is not so bad, really."

But after that Catherine realized it was like an hour glass, where the sand was running out. Soon only a handful of grains would remain and then there would be none. She felt totally panicked, they had tried and tried, searching and searching for a donor and none had been found.

But yet there must be one, she refused to admit it was not so, they only had to find this person. The terror flooded over her and now she knew she had to try harder, there must be a way forward.

That night she dreamed of Sophie again, perhaps it was her own daughter's talk which had brought the memory back; at the time she had felt relief that Sophie was giving Amelie comfort but no particular surprise. It was as if Sophie had a way of turning up when needed, even if she could not solve all the world's problems.

But, that night, as she fell asleep, there was the Sophie from her childhood, the girl of about six or eight in a white dress, she knew it was her first communion dress.

Sophie, with her small girl's solemn eyes, was saying to her. "Cathy, you need to find your true father, only he can help you."

It was like she was transported all those years back to that day in the desert when her mother had showed her the locket and together with Sophie guiding they had been rescued. It seemed now that she was returning again in a time of great need.

She remembered that her mother had given her that locket her for Christmas the year she left school. She knew where it was, sitting amongst her jewelry in the drawer. She took it out, hung it round her neck, determined that the next day her daughter should have it. It was she who now needed Sophie's help.

Part of her felt foolish, thinking a girl who had lived almost a century ago could help but another part felt strangely comforted at the thought of this ghostly presence.

Chapter 24 - Search for a Father

Next morning Catherine woke up with a clear purpose. She started by asking her mother if she thought that Sophie was still real, even after all these years.

Lizzie looked at her strangely. "Of course," she said, but why?"

Catherine replied, "Last night I dreamed about Sophie, she was telling me to find my true father. I don't know why, maybe it is just my desperate mind searching for any other options. It is so long ago since I remember Sophie, from when I was little, that, when I woke this morning, I started to wonder whether it was just my imagination. So I wanted to know what you think about her, Sophie."

Lizzie looked at Catherine seriously, "It is funny, but of late I have found myself thinking of her too. As you say, it may be coming from the same desperation you feel, but I know there was a real girl, Sophie, who lived in my bedroom almost fifty years before I did. I know she died when she was around eight years old. I know that from the time I visited her own Mum, Marie, when I saw her picture. Marie sort of told me that, not quite directly, but it was what she meant, that Sophie had died all those many years before I was born.

"And I have no doubt that Sophie talked to me before I was raped, warning me not to go with those men, even though I would not listen.

"You probably remember the story of all those years that I kept Sophie's locket sewed into the lining of my purse. I think I felt it was like a good luck charm.

"Then of course there was that time Sophie showed you the way to the water when we were in the desert. I have no doubt we would have both died then if not for that.

"So, even though I cannot explain how it can be that a little girl who lived half a century before me can communicate from beyond the grave, I have no doubt it is real, she is real and that she can talk to us at times as she did to both me and you.

"I also remember Sophie's own mother Maria's promise that she would help when I needed it. Perhaps that promise extends beyond you and me to Amelie too.

"Sophie has also been coming back into my mind over the last few days too, not talking to me, but in other ways making me remember her. I have told Amelie some of the stories about her from when I was little. It helps to pass the time and, when I talk of Sophie, Amelie's eyes light up.

Now, for Amelie, Sophie is real to her too, though whether that is just because she is imagining her from my stories, or experiencing her the way I did, I do not know. But now she is talking about her too and telling me that Sophie has become her friend.

"I find it pleases me that Amelie has found a person to be her friend and comfort her in this terrible time. But I am sure that is not why you asked, you know much of what I have told you now already. You were there in the desert too and it was you she actually spoke to on that day, not me.

"So why is she coming back to us all now, what is she trying to tell us about you needing to find your true father? Is it that she is saying that this man can help us, is that what you think?"

Catherine took a deep breath, her mother had always said before that the rape was something in her past that she did not need to think about, all that mattered was Catherine had been born and that fact made her glad.

But she knew that, despite this talk, it was still a painful memory for her mother; remembering the three men holding her down and doing this to her, a girl of only fifteen. But yet she had to go there. She had to ask her mother about it.

She said, "Mum, I hate to ask. But, for the first time in my life, I really do need to know. Do you have any idea which of the three men who raped you that night is my father?"

Her mother paused for a long minute before replying. It was as if her mind had suddenly conceived of a new possibility, an awful option that brought hope.

At last she said, "It is funny, I have never thought about it the way you just put it to me. I think I always felt that you were all of their child in that act and yet none of their child. To me that act was incompatible with fatherhood, its brutality and fatherhood could never sit together in my own mind.

"So, all my life, until the trial day when Martin went to jail with the other two, I refused to have that thought, that one of them really was your biological father. Robbie was a perfect father; he loved you from when you were a tiny baby just as much as any father could. So for me, in my mind, he became your actual father, no other father was needed to create your existence in my mind.

"But, on that day, the day when Martin was convicted, I went and sat next to Julie in the gallery. I told myself I was only there to support her, but it was more than that, I needed to see justice done with my own eyes.

"On that day another person was sitting near me in the gallery too, it was Martin's wife. As the trial proceeded I kept finding her eyes were on me, casting hateful glances towards me, as if she blamed me for all that had happened. I could feel her malice and I was glad to know it hurt her.

"Sitting beside her was a small girl, perhaps three years younger than you. What struck me about her was that she seemed to be the image of you at the same age.

"So, when I saw that girl who looked so like you, I was almost sure Martin was your father. I did not want to believe it. I would rather it had been one of the others, not that they were really better, but to me they seemed slightly less awful, more followers than the leader.

"Dan of course was Martin's clone, I remember the day he stood in my restaurant in Broome and gloated, both over what he had done and over what he intended to do again. His evil almost overwhelmed me, but it was just a copy of Martin's evil, more like a pale shadow.

"William I don't really know, he was an equal participant but I doubt I ever spoke more than two words to him in any conversation, before or after that night. Still he was a little more aloof and it was him that finally broke ranks and gave the evidence that convicted the others. So I have felt a little more fondness for him than the others since then, not much but a little. If I could choose the father I wished from the three it would be him.

"But I am fairly sure Martin was your father, based on seeing you in his little girl. But then, if it is Martin, that is of no help to you. He has been dead now for nearly ten years, though he does have children around your age. But then, perhaps, seeing you in his daughter could all be in my mind. It still could really be one of the others.

"I suppose we will have to try and find out."

Catherine said, "Yes, I do need to know, Amelie is fading so fast and there is so little time left to find a donor. It may be a futile hope but I need to know, at least to ask them to give me samples to test.

"Of course, if we can work out from the DNA testing who is the father, it may not help, this person may not be a match either, just the same as how Mathew and I are not matches. But I still need to know."

Lizzie said, "Of course you must know, we both must know for Amelie's sake. My father, when I was a little girl, used to tell me, when I really did not want to do something but the choice was even worse, that I was making a 'Devil's Choice'. This is our 'Devil's Choice'.

"I will ask Julie to get me the details of them and their families, she is good at that sort of thing. Then we can arrange to meet them and make our request. We must do it quickly as there is not much time."

Catherine looked directly at her mother, locking her eyes into hers. "It would be good if you would get those details from Julie. But then it is only for me to contact them. You have already done your part of the Devil's Choice in telling me what you know. It is now up to me to beg the man who is my father to help me, despite the evil he did to you."

Lizzie nodded her agreement, "Much as I hate to concede anything to these men you are right, it is more likely that they will help you, as someone who may be their daughter, rather than me as the person who helped to put them in jail.

"Martin's wife will hate me until the day she dies, and the others probably do too.

"But I do not envy you seeing this through, even though it must be done. I still cannot think of these men without the fear and loathing of that day rising up in me."

That day when Catherine came to the hospital to see her daughter she offered her the silver locket with Sophie's picture inside.

Amelie held it for a minute in her tiny, almost translucent hand, staring at it intently. Then she handed it back to her mother saying, "Thank you Mummy, but I have Sophie here with me. So I do not need her picture. I think you should keep it as it was a present to you."

Chapter 25 - First Meeting

It only took a day for Julie to come back with the details of all three men and their families.

Martin's wife, Marilyn and two children, a boy aged fifteen, named after his father, and a girl of thirteen named Rebecca, lived in a house in Newcastle near Nobby's Beach. The other child, Evelyn, aged nineteen, had come to Sydney but as yet they did not have an address for her. It was understood she was studying at New South Wales University and lived somewhere nearby.

Julie had placed a call from her firm to the mother, Marilyn, and found out she was at home over the next two days. So on the second day Catherine took the early morning train to Newcastle and took a taxi to the house, arriving about 9:30 am. She decided to arrive unannounced as she feared this lady would refuse to meet her if she gave her name.

A hard faced lady met her at the door, a lady with blond hair and once pretty features, but who had not aged well, already in her late thirties or maybe forties, she was overweight and her skin had sun damage.

Catherine gave her a bright smile, only to be met by a suspicious and guarded look.

Even though she doubted that this lady would have any idea of who she was there was already something unfriendly in her stare, perhaps it was the resemblance which Lizzie had said that she had to the daughter. At the front door Catherine said she needed to discuss a private matter and asked if she could come in to do so. Clearly reluctant the lady showed her into the formal drawing room and indicated a seat. No refreshments were offered.

Catherine launched into an explanation of how her daughter was sick and needed a bone marrow transplant to save her life. The woman looked perplexed. Then finally she got to the point that she thought that Martin could have been her father, she said that her mother was unsure but thought it was most likely to be him. As this came out she could see a nasty enjoyment spreading over this other woman's face.

"What did you say your name was, who is your mother?"

So there was no avoiding this information coming out. When Catherine answered the question there was a long pause, but nothing resembling sympathy showed on Marilyn's face.

Finally she spoke, "Well you have a nerve. How dare you come here and ask for my help? Your sluttish mother, having seduced my Martin, then tried to cry rape. She was a key person in destroying his business, our family reputation and sending him to jail where he was murdered.

"Despite all that you still come to me and ask for my help. I hope nothing saves your daughter and she dies an awful and painful death like my husband did. Not that Martin is likely to be the father, I am sure Lizzie had already slept with half the boys in Balmain before she flung herself at my Martin, when he was just trying to be kind to her. He never admitted to even sleeping with your slut mother. But yet you have the gall to come and ask for my help.

"What is it that you think I and my children ever could or ever would do to help you? Why did you ever come here anyway?"

Catherine felt shocked by this woman's viciousness; this was hatred towards her beyond anything she had imagined. Still she kept her resolve, determined not to lose the opportunity, if any existed.

"On the day your husband was sent to jail my mother was sitting in the public gallery near you. Sitting next to you was your oldest daughter. It struck my mother that your oldest daughter, who is three years younger than me, looks remarkably like me.

"After seeing your daughter, on that day, my mother was almost certain that Martin was in fact my father because of the family similarity between your daughter and me.

"So, if that is the case, and my mother has told me she is happy to give evidence to that effect, then we have good grounds to get a court ruling to compel your daughter to provide a sample for testing.

"If we are to go down that pathway of compulsion, rather than seeking cooperation, we would seek that all your children provide a sample, lest it be shown that another of Martin's children is the most suitable for a donor.

"So, whether you help or not, we would then know who the father was. We would be happy to tell the world of this fact, yet another proof of the violent behavior of your husband, confirming I am his daughter and your children are my half brothers and sisters.

"It seems to me somehow fitting that this awful man, your husband, who harmed my mother and who may even so be my own biological father, should be compelled to provide aid to my daughter if she is his own biological granddaughter, and to do this through his other children, even though he is not alive to enjoy the justice of the moment.

"I have not decided yet whether to do so, but if I do it will come through an order of the court. You may wish to advise your children, who may be my half-brother and sisters, of this likelihood."

As she spoke this she watched Marilyn carefully, wishing to gauge her reaction so as to help her decide.

Marylyn looked at her with a vicious contempt but also, once the testing word was said, with something like fear. "You must be joking; I hope you, your daughter and especially your mother, rot in hell. There is no way I will ever help any of you or allow my children to do so. Now get out of my house before I call the police and ask them to arrest you for trespass.

Catherine stood up and turned to leave. She knew this was hopeless, and felt that the words she had spoken were nothing but a hollow threat.

As she stepped around the chair to leave her eyes fell on three framed pictures on the mantel piece. One was of a young teenage girl and the second of a mid-teenage boy, neither looked like her. But the third was of a girl who looked not much younger than her, wearing a lovely dress, perhaps dressed for an end of school formal.

She was so like Catherine that it almost took her breath away, the resemblance was really striking, not in all ways, but there was an indefinable look that was just her, it could have been a photo of her taken around the time she got married; it was as if this girl was really herself, as if this picture captured the person in her own wedding photos.

Heedless of the mother Catherine walked over and picked the photo up, looking closely and saying. "I can see why Mum thought that Martin was my father; she is so like me, she really could be my sister."

The woman screamed in rage, "Get out, I told you to get out, how dare you compare yourself to my Martika; she is nothing like you, she is the image of her father."

Catherine found her fear of this woman had gone and in its place she had a hard rage. "I do not know if Martin was my father and, of all the three awful men who raped my mother, and of whom your vile husband was the instigator, I hope it is not him. But, as I said, I have been told that if needed I can get a court order and force all your three children to give a sample to see who matches my daughter best. When I show the judge a picture of your daughter, alongside a photo of me on the day I was married, I have no doubt he will grant an order compelling what I seek. So, if I need to, that is what I will do and, one way or another, I will find out."

As she spoke these words she saw the woman flinch. Something like real fear now sat alongside the anger and hatred in this woman's eyes. She wondered what this woman was afraid of in testing her daughter, was there a secret there she wanted not to share.

It gave Catherine an unfathomable thread of hope that there may be something more to help her here. And if she needed to she would pursue it to the bitter end, wherever that led.

Chapter 26 - Second Meeting

The following day Catherine was shown into the reception of the Long Bay Prison Hospital. She had already rung through yesterday afternoon, after her meeting with Marilyn, to arrange the visit.

She had been told that Dan Ashcroft was an extremely difficult and dangerous prisoner who often had to be forcibly restrained and she was likely to find this meeting difficult and confronting, she could sense the prison authorities would prefer this visit never occurred.

But for her there was no choice, it may be awful but she must see it through. Perhaps kindness and charm would work were threats failed.

But as she walked through the gates from the outside into the prison complex and surveyed the high walls with their razor wire topping, she felt as if she was descending into a version of hell, none of the nice house as a veneer to hide a monstrous person that she had been struck by yesterday. Here evil was in the air both within and without.

At first it was almost a relief, after entering the forbidden jail grounds, to step through the hospital doors where cleanliness, orderlies in white and brightly lit spaces seemed less bleak. Yet the cheerless sterility of the outside, an absence of any smiling faces or semblance of ordinary life permeated this place as well. But, as well, there was a sense of business like efficiency and people hardened against ordinary emotions which suffused the space. Despite the light filled clean surfaces, it was more hideous than the external barren walls and lifeless squalor.

She tried to block this from her mind as she was taken down the long corridor from the reception to the meeting place. She came into a room where a man, in pale track pants and a white long sleeve polo shirt, sat.

He looked relatively innocuous, like any other patient, and somehow cowed and pathetic. But, as he looked up, pure malice gleamed in eyes that seemed both knowing and mad. There was an evil shining from this person more terrifying than anything which came from Martin's wife. She gained an instant insight into the way her mother had felt that day when Dan Ashcroft had come to visit her in her restaurant in Broome. Now she understood, in a way she never had before, why her mother had just fled that day, without thought, to escape this awfulness.

All thoughts of pleading with this man for help drained out of the plug holes of her mind. Yet she must, even so.

She dropped her gaze as she took a deep breath and collected her thoughts. He began speaking before she could form her own words. "Who are you and what do you want?"

Then he peered more intently, his face showing recognition. "I know you; you are someone I met before. That's right, I met you as a small girl, all those years ago, at the school in Broome. You told me the way to your mother's house, how old were you then, maybe six, cute as a button and so very trusting.

"It was a big help to follow your directions and not to have to ask further. It was such a satisfaction to see the look of unexpected pleasure on your mother's face when she saw me, after you told me the way."

Catherine had forgotten her role in trusting this man, as a six year old child, giving the directions to her own house so he could find her mother. This memory was something she must have buried in a locker in her mind. It came flooding back, along with her mother's panicked flight, bringing Cathy with her, going far out into the desert to escape him.

She felt amazement that he could recognize her as an adult from last seeing her as a small child. But there was something calculated and clever in his madness, an ability to see clearly with different eyes which found only the details they sought out.

She decided to pick up where that conversation had left off all those years ago, hoping his mind still lived in that place as an escape from now.

"Yes I remember you and how I helped you. Now I am asking you to help me in return. My own little girl, who is even younger than I was on that day, needs your help. She needs to find my father and she wants to know if it is you. She needs you to give a sample for testing.

The man made an obscene cackle, like a feigned amusement, "Well, isn't she a sweet little thing to ask for help through you, she really should have come to ask me herself. I am afraid I must say no as I don't answer requests unless they come from the person who is making them.

"Though I suppose I could make an exception for you, seeing as you once were a sweet little girl too. But even for you I will not make a full exception, for me to help there is always price, everything comes with a price, even helping cute little girls, in fact especially helping cute little girls.

"So tell your little girl she must come and see me and ask me herself, or I will not agree. Perhaps she could give me a kiss on the cheek when she comes and asks, ever so nicely, If she does that then I will think about it. That is what all nice little girls should do.

"I like little girls; I have held and played with a lot of little girls, even touched them in private places when their Mummies and Daddies weren't looking. Yes I am happy to hold and cuddle your little girl that way too if she asks nicely enough. Perhaps if she lets me cuddle and touch her I will agree to give a sample, otherwise the answer is no."

At that moment Catherine could not bear this awful man any more, there was something so uncompromising in his vile madness. She could not bear for him to have been her father, or her daughter's grandfather. She really could not bear to allow herself to touch any part of him or have him touch any part of her or Amelie.

She knew, no matter how desperate she was, she had made a bad mistake in coming to see him. His pedophile's leer had polluted her inside and out. She would not let any part of this touch her daughter.

She could always seek a court order to have a sample forcibly taken from him to test whether he was her parent. But she could not bear the thought of finding out if it was indeed so, she understood her mother's desire that it be anybody but him, he was barely human and that human fragment was so twisted and perverted by evil that it had ceased to have a human soul even if the body still looked like that of a living person.

So she walked away from him with rage and despair in equal parts.

As she came back to the prison reception she was handed a message from an orderly in a white uniform. It said, "Please ring hospital, your daughter's breathing has got very bad."

She rang and talked to her Mum who told her since she had gone in this morning Amelie had deteriorated sharply, she was starting to have real difficulty with her breathing and they had diagnosed pneumonia. They had started a course of new antibiotics and put her back on oxygen. But they were very worried about how it might turn out.

It was not a good time for her to be away from her daughter's side. Patsy was also trying to arrange for Mathew to visit, lest Amelie continued to deteriorate.

Catherine left the prison and caught a taxi back to the hospital. Her heart was pounding and her hands were clammy as the fear escalated inside her, hoping this was not the end of all hope. She quickly made her way up to the ward.

Three doctors, two nurses and her mother stood in a circle round her daughter's bed, blocking her view. Then she saw Amelie in side profile; she had not looked her way.

Her daughter at first glance did not look too bad, though she was now being given oxygen; perhaps this had improved her breathing and colour and made her seem less sick.

Catherine looked at the clock, it seemed like a whole day had passed since she got up this morning, leaving early to go to the prison because they said this was the best time to meet Dan. It was only still eleven am.

She wondered why time seemed to have stopped. It was as if her whole life was running in slow motion. .

Her daughter looked up, "Mummy," she whispered, a happy but unworldly smile on her face, "what are you doing here, you are supposed to be at the prison, trying to find your father and my grandfather. You must go back and find him now."

Catherine came to her daughter and put her hand on her small forehead. It felt unnaturally hot, a fever was taking hold. Amelie took her hand in hers and pulled it away from her head, looking at her with flushed cheeks and over bright eyes.

"Mummy I know you have been looking and it is hard. But you must not stop now, you must keep looking for your father, Sophie says you must. That is the most important thing."

Cathy pulled her own Mum aside and asked her what she thought, it felt to her that it was like her daughter was sliding into a place from which there was no way back and she needed to stay by her side.

Yet Amelie was so clear and insistent that she must keep looking. It was like Amelie could see beyond the world in which they lived. As her body slid away it seemed her mind gained clearness far beyond the age and wisdom belonging to the person who lived within this tiny body.

Lizzie said. "The oxygen seems to have helped her breathing. Soon, with luck, the antibiotics will start to control the pneumonia. I think she is right. There is still one more man you must visit and ask; that is William. I am sure if you asked the prison they would arrange for you to see him as soon as you can get back today. You could be there in time for lunch, and be back here not long after if you need to.

Ring now and see if you can arrange it and, if you can, then go straight away. That way you will have at least done what Amelie is asking and she will be pleased by that. It may be that her child wisdom sees something we do not, we must not waste that.

Meantime I will ring the prison if any further problems with Amelie develop and you need to hurry back.

Chapter 27 - Moment of Truth

Catherine walked out of the room where William sat; having heard and agreed to his demand that she bring her mother in to see this man, her former rapist. It felt so wrong, knowing that she must accede to yet one more despicable request.

She knew she now had only one roll of the dice left, and along with it was the knowledge that it may be too late anyway. She had a sick feeling that everything she did was destined for failure. It felt as if the effort would overwhelm her to keep going. She just wanted to be with Amelie.

She found her way back into the prison office, so as to ring her mother who was sitting in the hospital by Amelie's bedside, and ask her to leave her daughter and come here instead. She prepared her mind to make the request. It was hard to think coherently, let alone to talk.

This man, William, had also been unbelievably awful, the fact that he could suggest having sex with a person who could be his own daughter had rocked her to her core, the way he had talked about her mother had been hideous, even though he had in the end admitted he had raped her. Then the demand from him to bring her daughter, she knowing that, with her daughter's immunity shot to bits and with the hospital struggling to control her current bout of pneumonia with high powered antibiotics, there was no way she could be moved from her hospital bed, where the continuous drip fed her life sustaining fluids and nutrition, now that she could no longer eat. So that had been an impossible demand.

It was all too hard; she wanted to walk away from this place full of awful people. But still her mind willed her to keep going. She prayed that the hospital would somehow manage to keep her daughter alive, even for a few more days and buy some chance that a bone marrow donor could be found.

After this man William had talked about her mother in that awful way, nearly as bad as the way Dan had talked even though this man did not strike her as mad, she had felt that she had used all her chances and lost. And yet, just at the end, when he had agreed to her proposal to just bring her mother and a photo of her daughter instead she thought she had detected something more decent buried deep, a place of compassion.

Lizzie had told her several times over the last week that she had to prepare her mind for her daughter to die, to allow her to go with grace and dignity. But she could not. She refused to give up while even one thread of hope remained, however tenuous.

She was so angry at God that he had allowed it to come to this; she knew there was someone out there with power over the Universe and the people in it. Sophie had shown her that, long ago, when she had saved her and her mother's life. And the dream she had of Sophie, a few days past, when all else seemed lost, had seemed to suggest that there was still some hope if she could only find her true father. But that other despicable man, Dan, had refused to help. Dan was nothing more than an evil and degenerate idiot tied to a bed in the psychiatric ward. But he still had enough knowledge to pervert and refuse her request to allow a sample to be taken to see if his tissues were a suitable match for his daughter.

She knew she could obtain a court order to have it done, that was what the lawyer said, and it was the same with Martin's children. But she had run out of time for that or, at least, she had to try this other possible father first, in the event that he could help without further delay.

The hourglass holding the few remaining grains of her daughter's life was so nearly empty, there was no time for any further tries, unless a miracle happened and her daughter stabilized. So she knew realistically this man was her last hope, this despicable man, her mother's rapist, someone who had leered at her as he recalled the pleasure that this brutal act had given him.

All these thoughts were swirling in her mind as she walked to the phone and picked it up.

Still this one thing remained, to ask her mother to come, to drop everything, leaving little Amelie all alone while she returned to meet this man and subject herself to his awful scrutiny while he leered at her. It really was a devil's choice.

But while any hope remained of saving her daughter's life she would do whatever it took, no limits. She so wished Mathew was here to help her, not locked up by himself. She was so tired of trying to fight the whole world on her own.

She steeled herself and took another deep breath, picked up the phone and starting dialing the number to get her mother. The nurse picked up and she asked to speak to her mother, saying who she was. She knew from her mother's first words, it was there too in her tone of voice, that there was a new and more immediate problem to deal with.

"Oh my God, Cathy I am so glad you rang. Amelie has gone downhill really fast in the last hour and a half since you left.

"I think we are losing her. You need to come back to the hospital as soon you can. She is going blue, despite the oxygen, and every breath is a struggle. The doctors think she has only a few hours to live."

Cathy stood there holding the phone in shock, it was past time to seek any help; she must go back to her daughter's side and help her make her peace with God.

She said, "OK Mum, I am coming."

She turned to go, there was a man walking fast down the hall way towards her. She recognized him as one of the warders from the cell.

The man said to her, "He has asked to see you again; I think he has decided to help."

She felt torn, she should just leave; her mother had as good as said it was too late. But there was still a tiny thread of hope if this man could help, she refused to surrender it. She nodded and followed the warder back to the room.

This man, William was still sitting there. But something indescribable was different. She looked at him closely. She could have sworn she could see the traces of tears in his otherwise hard eyes.

He said, "Before you go, I have a favour to ask, just a favour, not a condition to helping you. Could you tell me something about this little person, your daughter, that you want me to help, just something about her, anything really?"

Catherine was thrown, she did not know what she was expecting, but it was not this. She thought and the words came. "She loves a red car. She got it for Christmas and barely got out of it until she got sick. Now, even though she is too sick to get out of bed, she can barely breathe, we keep it beside her hospital bed and she still looks at it every day and smiles.

She heard a muffled noise behind her. She looked around, the warder was crying.

She remembered. She had a photo of her daughter, sitting in the red car on Christmas Day, in her purse. She took it out and handed it to the man. "That is for you to keep, something to know her by, perhaps she is your granddaughter. That photo was taken last Christmas, just before she got sick.

The man sat there looking at the picture, slowly something in his face crumpled until tears were streaming down his cheeks. "She looks just like my mother and my sister when they were little; there are photos of them in the house where I used to live. It is a long time since I have seen them but I still remember."

Catherine fixed her eyes on him and bored them into him, determined to make this moment count. "So, you will try and help me save the life of your granddaughter?"

The man nodded mutely.

Suddenly Catherine remembered what her mother had said, that it was too late, that her daughter was dying, she was unlikely to make it through until tonight.

She shook her head, anger flaring, looking at this man who had made his offer too late. "Well thank you for your offer but I am afraid it is past time to help. When I went out before to ask my mother to come here she told me my daughter was dying, she told me to come back to the hospital to hold her in my arms one last time while she yet lives, as she will probably be dead by tonight. She has pneumonia as well as lungs full of cancer cells. The doctors told me the only hope to save her life was a bone marrow transplant. We have all searched for a month and been unable to find someone.

"So, as a last act of desperation, I came to ask you to be tested to see if you were suitable and, if you were, to be the donor, even though your only role in my birth was to rape my mother.

"So thank you for your kind offer, but it seems I will have to decline it, the time for helping is past."

She turned to leave. The warder started to unlock the door, his hands shaking as he fumbled with the keys.

A voice behind her called out. "Please wait, just for another minute."

She turned to face him, anger still flaring along with contempt. "Yes?"

"It may be nothing, but in my free time I have been studying medicine and things like that. I have read of a technique called white blood cell transfusion, which is used on cancer patients when their immunity is gone. They take white cells from a suitable donor and give them to the sick person and sometimes they can help fight off the infection and help also kill the cancer cells. Perhaps, if I could give some blood, they could try that. Then, if that works and controls the pneumonia, they can test me to see if I am suitable for a bone marrow donor."

It was something that Catherine had heard the doctors talk about, experimental and last ditch. They had dismissed it as pointless without a bone marrow transplant as, at best, it would buy a few days. But perhaps it was something.

She looked steadily at the man, the rage gone. "Thank you for that, I will tell the doctors and see what they say, better still I will ring before I leave and ask them."

She went back to the phone and got put through to the oncologist and told him what had been said. She could almost imagine the cogs in his brain turning over as the silence continued, then he spoke.

"Well it is something and there is nothing else, it may at least help control the infection in her lungs and buy some time, as the antibiotics seem not to be working.

"Can you arrange for me to talk to the prison superintendent and I will see what I can arrange. We could ask the prison hospital to collect the blood and you could bring it back in an ambulance."

So it was that, in another half an hour, she was sitting in the front seat of the prison ambulance, siren blaring. It pushed its way through crowded city streets until it came to Camperdown. On her lap sat a plastic bag with a pint of this man's blood, bright and red.

Catherine found herself praying as they drove, for what she knew not, not for her daughter's life, that seemed an impossible hope, but at least for something good to come out of this awful place where she had been.

She came to the hospital, handed over the blood and rushed up the corridors to the ward where Amelie lay, propped up in her own mother Lizzie's arms.

Amelie still was blue but seemed comfortable. She smiled at her mother with a beatific smile and said. "Mummy, Grandma has been telling me more about her friend Sophie, from when she was a little girl, the time she rescued you both in the desert. Now Sophie is talking to me, inside my head, telling me not to be frightened as she will look after me. She is also saying you have found my Grandpa, so thank you for looking."

Five minutes later a nurse came in with the blood bag saying. "We have checked the blood type and it matches, so the doctor has suggested that, rather than taking the time now to separate the white cells, we give her the whole blood. She is already anaemic and struggling for air so the extra red blood cells may help too."

So they connected the blood pack to the drip and they sat there with Amelia, telling more stories about their shared friend Sophie while the blood ran in, drip by drip. In three hours Amelie was no worse, maybe a bit pinker, in five hours her breathing seemed a bit better, still the blood kept running, drip by drip, slower now.

Cathy found herself shaking with fatigue, she had not eaten all day, but she realized that tonight there was still one more thing she must do. She must go and see Mathew and try and make him understand that he must stop fighting the whole world and come and add his bit towards helping his daughter.

She walked outside and asked a taxi to take her to the Kirkbride Building in Callan Park, Rozelle.

Chapter 28 - Mathew

It was coming up to ten o'clock at night and she knew she was pushing her luck to try and see someone at this late hour, but she knew she could be very persuasive when she needed to be.

She rang the bell, over and over. Finally a grumpy orderly came down to see who it was. Before the man had a chance to slam the door closed she wedged her foot inside.

He said, "What do you want so late at night, surely you realise that visiting hours finished over three hours ago."

She said, "I am Catherine, Mathew Jamison's husband. I need to see my husband, I will call the governor if I need to, but my daughter is dying and her father needs to come with me to see her, to hold her one last time and say goodbye."

There was something in the fierceness of her voice that silenced the man, he looked almost ashamed. "Yes of course you must see him. I will come up and unlock the door to his room. He should be in bed but I doubt he is asleep, he often stays awake half the night making his plans for a miracle to cure her or for revenge. Sometimes, if he gets too crazy, they have to give him a needle.

Catherine hardened her mind; it was just one more awfulness. She would see it through. The man unlocked the lock with his key and then knocked. "Mathew, you have a visitor."

The door opened from the inside. He was standing there in a dirty dressing gown, face gaunt and unshaved. But his eyes lit up with delight for an instant when he saw her, before reality dawned.

"I suppose you have come to tell me that my daughter is dead, poisoned to finish her off by those evil men, those doctors with their poison drugs are no better than the people who sprayed me with poison, killers the whole lot of them."

She looked at this man that she loved, even with the madness in his eyes and started to cry, she had not let herself really cry for months, she had forced herself to hold it together and try to be strong for the sake of her daughter.

"Oh Mathew, I need you to help me not to fight with me. I can't do this on my own anymore. I have tried to be brave and fight the world but now I am too tired, I just can't do it without you.

"Our daughter is not dead but she probably will be in a day or two and I need you to come and see her again, to hold her in your arms again and give her the comfort that only you can give. I will not let her die without you holding her one last time."

The sobs overwhelmed her and she stood there with her face in her hands, crying as if her heart would break.

For a minute Mathew stood next to her, looking at her in anguish but uncertainty. Then he shuffled over and wrapped his arms around her and held her, stroking her hair and trying to comfort her like a child.

She sobbed as she clung to him and he held her too, loving having this woman back in his arms, somehow helping her took away his own pain.

Gradually her crying stopped and now she looked up at him steadily. "Will you come?

"Yes, I will come, I know now that I have failed you both and must stop running away by blaming others and hiding behind my anger. So yes, I must come and hold my little girl again and comfort her. At the same time I will try and comfort you as you have for me in the past."

Catherine turned to him again and said, "There is something I must tell you from today, we must neither of us let ourselves hope, but it is something. I have found a man who may be able to help her, to be the donor she needs to save her life. He is in Long Bay Jail for rape and murder but he says he thinks he is my father; he told me our daughter is the image of his mother and his sister, so he thinks he must be the one. Just when I had seen him, soon after lunch time, my mother rang to say Amelie was dying, she would not see out the day.

"Then this man gave her his blood and by tonight her blueness had gone and she was pink again. She has pneumonia still and is very sick but if she can recover enough from that then perhaps they can give her enough drugs to kill all the cancer cells and then, if this man is a match, he can give her new healthy bone marrow to let her live again.

"It is not certain, but it is something with more hope than anything since she got sick the second time. So we must both hope and pray. And even if it is not enough and she dies, yet still we must both hold and comfort her and each other as well.

"So tomorrow you must come with me and take her and hold her and tell her that you love her. That is all you can do, that is all any of us can do. Then we must trust the rest to God.

Mathew nodded, he was past fighting God and man too, he knew she was right, loving his daughter and his wife was all he could do, he must let go of the other.

Catherine turned around; the orderly was still standing in the hallway looking in. She turned to him and said. "It is OK; I will stay with my husband tonight. You can lock the door if you need to. Tomorrow we will both go to our child."

Chapter 29 - A Chance

Catherine awoke in the early morning dawn. For a second she wondered where she was, she felt safe and happy. Then she realised that Mathew's arms were around her and it felt so good. Last night they had loved each other with their bodies for the first time in months.

That simple act had been like the lancing of a boil, it had let the poison out of both their souls. In its place something good had begun to grow again.

Catherine knew her daughter's life still hung in the balance, there was every chance that they would be burying her inside a week and while part of her quailed at that thought another part of her knew now she had done everything she could and that this was in God's hands now.

Yesterday, when Amelie had spoken of her friend Sophie, with a wisdom far beyond her three and a half years, saying her friend would look after her, another wall had broken inside her. She knew Sophie had saved her and her mother all those years ago and, in her mother telling Amelie that story, a simple door to faith and belief had been opened.

That did not mean Amelie would live, but it gave her comfort that she would be cared for and safe, even beyond the grave. That was a gift far beyond the power of most people to give.

And for her, equally precious, she had her husband and the man that she loved back. He had told her, after their love making and before they had slept in the dawn, that this was the first night in longer than he could remember how he was not haunted by demons in his dreams, that feeling her need had restored his own self, because he realised he had something he could give.

But, beyond even that, she had hope for her daughter's survival. As the colour had flowed back into her veins and her breathing eased yesterday she had felt in the presence of something miraculous, a miracle that at the time had seemed beyond grasping, but as if this other man's act of giving his blood had carried something more, like it was the first decent thing he had ever done and in that salvation he was also giving new life to another person.

She pulled herself up short. Best not to let flights of fancy run away in her mind. She did not even know for sure that he would be a suitable donor, all she had so far was recognition of a photo and a blood match, a tissue match was vastly more improbable.

But yet, when one is in the presence of a miracle then faith is all that remains; so she must hold onto her faith and believe that what seemed impossible less than a day ago was indeed possible. So she allowed herself to smile, she had faith again and with it came an ability to have joy in life.

She realised Mathew was awake and looking at her intensely. "You are smiling he said. It is so long since I have seen you really smile. I had forgotten how beautiful it was."

She nodded, "I have my belief back, my belief in God and in the goodness of life. In all their lives most people never witness a miracle, in the last day I have witnessed four. They say that three of anything is more than enough; four is truly a gift from God.

Mathew looked at her inquiringly.

She continued. "Yesterday morning I was watching my daughter die, desperate and hopeless. To save her I went and begged the most evil man I knew, my mother's rapist and a convicted murderer who smiled while he killed another man without remorse and yesterday had smiled when he remembered what he did to my mother. I knew I was in the presence of evil and yet I begged.

'Then, when I showed this man the picture of our Amelie, the first miracle happened. He sat there looking at her with tears rolling down his face. In her picture he recognised his own mother and sister and more than that he recognised the evil in what he had done.

"In that moment I knew both that I had found my real father and that he would help me. At first it made me hate him more, I would not allow him to have redemption through crying, it was too easy for him, it was too late. My daughter was past help, so the offer was a meaningless gesture. But that remorse opened something good inside him and with that desire to help came the next part of that miracle, the knowledge that his blood could help and the willingness to give it, to do something real not just feel regret.

"The second miracle was when I returned to hospital. My daughter was still dying but something had happened inside her which had taken away all her fear and had given her peace and comfort. My mother was telling Amelie the story of Sophie, my friend and how she saved my mother and my life in the desert. As I listened I remembered so clearly how Sophie had told me not to worry when we sat alone and thirsty, waiting to die. She did not promise me that we would live, she simply told me not to worry or be frightened as she would mind both of us.

"In that moment, when I saw Amelie's beatific face, it was as if she was already with the angels and Sophie was caring for her. So I knew that, no matter whether Amelie lived or died, I did not need to be afraid for her anymore.

"The third miracle was when I watched that blood flow into Amelie, drip by drip, hour by hour and suddenly my dying daughter was not dying anymore, something in that blood had given her new life. It may only be a temporary reprieve but the new life is real.

"The final and, for me, the most important miracle was, last night, to come here, expecting to find in you only rage and madness, but needing you all the more. Instead I found love returned.

"So now I cannot help but smile. Four miracles should be more than enough. But yet I want and believe there can be one more. That our daughter can receive this man's own bone marrow cells and, with them and the other drugs, they can kill the cancer and she can survive."

Mathew put his arms around her and held her close. "I too have had my own miracle; that you came back to me in need. In the past you have been so strong that there was nothing I could give you. Last night was the first time you have ever truly and totally needed me, just me. In that place something inside me was healed, the hate and rage was gone. I know my daughter needs me too and that is good and I will give it to her.

"But, most important was your own need, it finally brought us to the place where you were not strong enough on your own.

"I do not have your faith that our daughter can be cured; I have lived too many to times with failure for belief. Yet it is enough for me to feel your hope and live in your hope."

Chapter 30 - Last Roll of the Dice

Catherine and Mathew came into hospital about eight o'clock to find Amelie sitting up in bed and looking better than she had in more than a week. Lizzie was asleep in the chair next to her bed.

When Amelie saw her Dad she let out a whoop of delight. "Daddy, I knew you would come back. Mummy said she was going to get you and Grandma was sure you would come and see me, and Sophie told me you would come too. I am so happy now that everyone is here."

Mathew picked her up and cradled her in his arms. There was almost nothing of her now, just a little round head with a few sprigs of hair trying to grow and a wasted body. He was shocked at how thin she had grown, and felt remorse at selfishly neglecting her for the last two months to chase shadows in search of revenge.

He stroked her head as he cuddled her, saying. "I love you my pet and am so happy to see you again.

She ran her own little fingers though his hair and said. "I love you too Daddy, but of course you already know that. And I know everything will be all right now you have come back. Sophie promised me that as well."

He hugged her as if she was a porcelain doll which would break at a puff of wind. She felt so incredibly precious.

Yet, as he felt her feather weight and heard her wheezing and the rattle in her lungs, the terror gripped him too, it seemed impossible that she had lived so long let alone that she could survive any more. Part of him just wanted her suffering to be over and let her die in peace.

But then, as he thought that thought, he looked at her bright face, so full of life, and at his own Catherine's face, still daring to hope. He knew he must fight on and help keep the hope alive too.

Half an hour later a troupe of doctors came in. They had arranged to have William checked into the prison hospital and two of them had gone over to examine him, to take samples to determine whether his tissue would match Amelie's and also to check for any signs of diseases which threatened her.

Last night the laboratory had worked back late processing all the samples, as they all knew the clock was fast running down.

This far all seemed fine. It was likely William would be a suitable donor; finally, after more than 100 people tested, it looked like they had found someone suitable.

The tests would be completed late today and tonight William would be transferred to a secure bed in a hospital here.

At first the prison had been reluctant to allow him to be transferred, but Amelie's doctors had been insistent. They needed him right here on hand to have the minimum delay between extracting his cells and giving them to Amelie.

When all the test results were in this evening, if they confirmed a suitable match, Amelie would be scheduled to go for a first round of radiation treatment tomorrow, to kill as many of the cancer cells as possible, followed by a high dose of chemotherapy in her drip to start killing any surviving cancer cells. Then, the next day she would receive a second dose of radiation as a last ditch attempt to kill any remaining cancer cells.

In the process these treatments would kill all her own bone marrow cells. Then in three days, when the anticancer drug was flushed out of her body by the saline drip, they would start to give William's cells. To do this they would give William an anaesthetic and harvest these cells from the bone marrow in his hips. Then they would take these cells and run them into Amelie through a central venous catheter, slowly flowing these new and healthy cells into her body through her blood and hoping they would settle and start to multiply in her own bone marrow.

Normally they would have given William a treatment to boost his own bone marrow but that meant delaying the start of the killing her cancer cells. It was a race against time and time was not on her side to delay.

They would have also liked to get her stronger, to feed her up, but one look at the X-Ray of her lungs and it was clear there was no time for that either, already the cancer had more than half filled them. So tonight they must pray that all the tests came up right and tomorrow they would begin a last and desperate roll of the dice.

When the doctor had finished giving them all a detailed description of the process from here he paused and took a deep breath. He looked at them all seriously and said, "I just need to be sure you all understand the consequence if this fails. There is no way back.

"Once we have started this treatment if the bone marrow does not take Amelie will surely die, she will have no immunity and be unable to make blood cells or other things such as the platelets that stop her bleeding. Within a week, or two at the most, it will be over for her.

"We can give her transfusions to cover her for a few days but after that it is up to her. So you need to know that before you decide. And you must also know this treatment we will give her will also make her really sick as well, it will kill many healthy cells in her body, cells in her hair and skin and lungs. So for a few days she will be even sicker than she is now and she already has so few reserves on which to live.

"So the treatment may well kill her, even sooner than the cancer does. Having been so weakened by the cancer makes her a far from an ideal patient on which to use this procedure. Some of my colleagues are saying I should advise you against trying it; the risks are too great in her condition. "The chances of success would have been much higher if we had found a donor a month ago.

"You do not have to decide until all the results are in. So far the results are encouraging but we are still waiting on two further tests.

Only if they match as well can we be definite that the procedure is indicated.

You need to weigh this all up over the next few hours so that when the results are in you can make this decision. I expect to know by ten pm tonight, what all the results are."

When the doctor finished his long speech, Mathew and Catherine paused before replying, each waiting for the other to say something They both wanted to say yes, to take the offered hope, but they knew they were deciding on whether their daughter lived or died, acting as if they were God. It seemed such a huge step to take. They took each other's hands and looked at one another, neither wanting to speak first, together trying to weigh it all up.

It was Lizzie who broke the silence. "Doctor, I am convinced Amelie would have died yesterday but for that transfusion, she hovered in that place of crossing over. Everyone said we were losing her. I could bear that when there was no hope.

"But we will lose her anyway, today or tomorrow or perhaps in a week or two if we do not try. We have tried everything else and this is the last chance to stop the cancer and save her life. You say she may well die even with the treatment. I can live with that, I can bury her with love if I must. But I could not live with myself if we did not try.

"My daughter has been given the Devil's Choice, to beg the man who raped me all those years ago to save her daughter's life. This she did yesterday and with that awful choice she bought hope. I will not allow her to make another Devil's Choice today, to take it on herself to decide whether her daughter lives or dies.

"I will decide for her if I must. But I would like her husband, Mathew, to decide. I say he must share the Devil's Choice.

Lizzie walked over to Mathew and took his hands, pulling him to face her. "I think we both know that Catherine has done enough; already she has made one impossible choice. I would like you to make this choice. I will choose if I must, but I think this choice now belongs to you. You must choose which path to take and with it take responsibility for whether your daughter lives or dies, it must rest on your shoulders."

Mathew looked at her and nodded, then he looked back at Catherine, she nodded too, as if to say it was now for him alone. He looked at his daughter, sitting on her bed in the far corner of the room, playing with a doll, seemingly unaware of what they were doing.

Now he knew with clarity, he must take the hope brought at such a high price, he must accept his own Devil's Choice, regardless of whether his daughter lived or died from the choice.

He turned to the Doctor and said, "I choose the chance of life, I choose the treatment."

Lizzie and Cathy both nodded.

Suddenly Amelie turned to him and gave him a flashing smile. "Thank you Daddy, Sophie says you made the right choice."

Chapter 31 - Late in the Night

It was after ten in the night when all the results of the matching were in.

It was good but not good enough.

It was the best match they had found so far but still there were problems. The doctors were saying it was an even bet whether they should go ahead. Three of the four HLA genes were a good match, including the Melanesian one, but the other gene was only a partial match. It was not terrible but it was likely that any transplant would also need heavy doses of anti-rejection drugs and they came with significant side effects, they themselves harmed the immune system, which they were trying to rebuild with the transplant.

It was a bitter disappointment when all had seemed so promising. In the end the medical advice was to try and check the match some other ways, try things which would indicate whether this partial match really would be a real problem, and once this was done they could decide.

However the good news was Amelie seemed much better; it was as if the white cells from William had some special property that was making her better even if they were less than perfect as donor cells. William was now being kept in a high security ward on the floor below and could remain there on standby for another day or two if needed.

The time was approaching eleven pm. Amelie was sleeping soundly and they were thinking they too should go home and sleep. The desk phone at the nurse's station rang. The nurse passed it to Catherine. It was a request that she come to meet with William, he had asked to see her; he wanted to know about the match.

She came into his room with a security escort. He was sitting on his bed, reading the paper and looking a little pale and tired, as if the uncertainty was affecting him too.

William asked her how she and her daughter were going and if she knew the test results yet.

She nodded her head, "Yes the results are in."

"And?" he asked her, seeking more.

Despite her disappointment with the result she felt she still had hope, Amelie seemed much improved even if it was a temporary respite and he had done what he could.

Catherine smiled at him and he returned her smile, even if a bit unsure. He asked her what all the results were again.

Now she told him truthfully, that it was good but not perfect, the match was three and a half out of four; that they probably would still need to go ahead as it was the best option they had though they would really have liked to get a four out of four match score.

William looked at Catherine intently. "Perhaps there is one other thing you should know, I have spent the day hoping I was the right person but also trying to think of alternatives if I am not. There is still my sister and my mother, and my sister has three children. I am sure that any of them would help if I asked, even though none have spoken to me for more than ten years. They are all good people and would want to help. But there is someone else who I think is the most likely match.

"From what you told me it appears that you have sought help from all three of us who could be your father, not just from me. In doing so I imagine you will have been to visit Marilyn, Martin's former wife, and I doubt that she would have been helpful.

"When her oldest daughter, Martika, was little I saw her a lot, Martin and Dan were my friends, after a fashion. So I was like an uncle to this girl, she called me Uncle Will.

"You have probably not met her but I have seen her many times and she is the image of you, so alike you that anyone who saw you together would say you are sisters.

"There is a reason for that. In fact you are sisters, half sisters at any event, the reason for that is that I am her real father.

"It happened when Martin was away setting up his new company. He and Dan were away together for a month and I was left in charge of the Newcastle operation. Marilyn and Martin were only recently married when he went away. After a few days Marilyn started dropping in to the office where I was working.

"One day she stayed until late, after that others had left for the day When they were gone she brought a drink in for me and invited me to come to her place for dinner as she was alone by herself. Within five minutes of being back at her place we were in bed together. After that for the next three weeks until the day before Martin came home every night she came to my place and stayed with me.

"I think she knew that Martin could not keep his pants on when he went away and it was her way of getting her own back. Plus I think she was lonely and found Martin poor company, she and I talked for most of each night. I liked her and she seemed to like me. She made me promise never to tell Martin, she was scared of him.

"A couple months later, she announced she was pregnant. Martin was very lovey dovey with her after he returned though Dan told me that they had other women almost every night they were away, he was gloating, as if to make me jealous. I just laughed and said nothing, remembering how I had spent my nights.

"So I wondered then if Martin was really the father or whether the child was mine, it seemed almost too quick from when he returned and I doubt it was from before he went away.

"One day, three months later, I ran into Marilyn alone and asked her. She admitted I was the father, but told me I must never tell Martin or Dan or she would be in terrible trouble.

"So I never did, but every time Marti, named for her father, called me Uncle William I knew I was really her father and Martin was really the Uncle. But I have kept Marti and Marilyn's secret up until now.

"I have also wondered if Martin was the father of the other two and somehow I doubt it. None of his children look like him. Plus, from the way Marilyn talked about him it sounded like he was a dud in bed with her, she said he needed school girls or ones he paid for to get it up.

"But that is Marilyn's secret, though I am sure she does not want any of her children tested in case it comes out they are all from different fathers. So I have written her a letter to remind her of what I know."

Catherine shook her head in amazement, It all made a strange sense and it was almost as if she had known from the picture she saw that day that this girl and her were related

William now handed Cathy an envelope saying, "I think you need to keep trying to find a better donor than me. So I suggest you take this letter and arrange it be delivered to Marilyn. It simply gives her a choice, to willingly allow her daughter to be tested, and keep her secret or to have me tell the world and with the end result that her daughter will know the truth and may choose to be tested herself, not to mention what may come out if her other children are tested too.

"When Marti was little she was a sweet and kind natured girl. I have been told she is still a kind natured person. I think she would help if asked. I know it does not guarantee success but, if I was a betting man, I would bet on Marti being the donor you need."

The next day Julie arranged for a legal courier to deliver this letter to Marilyn. William said he had given her twenty four hours to decide before he acted.

The following day the phone rang for Catherine when she was at the hotel. It was the hospital saying they had a Marti in reception and she had heard a donor was needed for their daughter Amelie. She wanted to be tested to see if she was suitable.

Catherine rushed to the hospital, determined to meet this woman who was her half-sister and ask her herself. She found her in reception, waiting for oncologist to examine her. It was the strangest feeling, walking up to a person who looked almost as if she was looking at herself in the mirror. On seeing her Marti gave a delighted smile and came and took her hand, saying, I have been to see my Uncle in prison and know the real story. You do not need to ask for my help, I am your daughter's aunt after all. Perhaps in a small way I can help make retribution for what was done to your mother all these years ago.

So they sat together for the next two hours as all the tests were done. And then Catherine brought Marti home to the hotel to meet Mathew, Lizzie and Patsy. Together they all sat and waited until the results were in.

This time the test match was four out of four.

Chapter 32 - A Month Later

A month passed, Catherine and Mathew finally had their little girl back from hospital. She was alive but painfully thin, her face and body not much more than angles and bones, hollow cheeks, stick arms and legs, hair a thin fuzz on her head of a faded fawn colour.

Between one and two weeks after the treatment there had been many days when they had thought that she would not see the morrow, the drugs and radiation had made her so sick, giving her violent diarrhoea and vomiting of pitiful drops of bile coloured liquid; all her nutrition had come by drip.

The doctors said it was not only the toxic effect of the drugs but also that her own body cells were struggling to repair and that there were so many dead cancer cells in her body that also had to be broken down. So both these and the effects of the drugs on poisoning her body had to overcome, but at the same time they feared that her body had lost its ability to recover. Fortunately she was small and Marti was big and so they had been able to keep transfusing her regularly with blood and white cells until gradually her body took over, a couple times the doctors had joked almost morbidly, that Amelie was like a vampire being fed with this Marti's blood.

But they had refused to give up hope; they had washed Amelie's tiny body each day to keep it clean. They had stroked and cuddled her and she had rewarded them when sufficiently aware with her delightful smiles, though sometimes it had felt she was closer to being an angel than a living person. Each night, when she had gone to sleep, they wondered whether she would still be breathing in the morning.

But she had kept weeing copious amounts from all the fluids in the drip and she had not got jaundiced. The doctors said these were good signs that her kidneys and liver were still working. Her heartbeat also stayed strong; with so little else of her it reverberated through her body.

In the third week Amelie started to be able to take small drinks and bland food, a little bit of mashed banana was the first thing she had kept down. By the end of that week they stopped fluids and blood transfusions and took the drip line out.

Last week she was much brighter and more wakeful, starting to play with her dolls again, telling them stories about her and Sophie and what they were doing together, sometimes putting the rest of her family into the stories too. The first signs of new downy hair started to appear on her head, as well. It was wonderful evidence that her body was doing its own repair at last.

Each day since she had become brighter and hungrier though there was little evidence of all the food she was eating in her pitifully thin body. At the end of last week she had taken her first steps again on her own legs, after two months in a bed. At first she had wobbled and held her Daddy's hand, but then she had walked about with confidence.

Now they were sure her body was repairing itself, perhaps it would never be as big and strong as it once would have been; perhaps she would never have children of her own. But every day, after that, she was their own walking and talking miracle.

They had watched anxiously as she started to become better for any signs of the tumours returning. Each week they did a blood smear though, at first, her blood was so full of donor cells that it was impossible to tell. But there were no lumps at all and, on a chest X-Ray last week, all the tumours in her chest were gone and her lungs were clear. Last week too there were new white and red cells in her blood which had definitely come from her, so it seemed that the bone marrow transplant had taken.

Next week would be her three and a half birthday, only a month late. It seemed like an eternity since that happy day by the harbour when she had turned three, a month ago it had seemed impossible that she would be here and smiling on this day. They had received so many cards and gifts from well-wishers that had taken this little girl to her heart that the following Sunday they were having a special birthday party for her in the hotel courtyard. They had invited staff and well-wishers to come along and it was their way of saying thank you for all the support.

Now they could feel a possibility of a fourth birthday and others beyond, though they were determined to only take one day at a time and live in each day.

Tomorrow Lizzie was flying home for a month, she and Mathew had no words that could ever express their gratitude to her Mum, she and Robbie had put their lives on hold and barely been together since late April when the relapse occurred, he keeping the business running in Broome and caring for Catherine's own brother and sister there, her Mum her almost constant companion and support.

Then there was her Gran who had helped equally in her own way, taking over management of the hotel for her when Mathew had been taken away, managing the staff and doing the rosters, pouring beers when required and telling jokes with the customers to maintaining the happy pub atmosphere despite the turmoil swirling around her.

She and Mathew had tried to thank them over the last month as they started to find time, but both had brushed this aside, they were family and that is what families did.

Catherine also realised that accepting this all gratefully was part of life's learning for her, she had been so independent and determined to do her own thing, and only when her own need had become overwhelming had there really been space for Mathew back in her life, it was like her need for him, more than anything else, had healed his mind.

She had one really important thing that she now needed to do. She needed to find some way to thank this man who was her true biological father for his gift of life. He had been returned to jail the day after they had decided not to use his bone marrow and she had never seen him herself since that night when he told her the secret of Marti.

Marti and Catherine had continued on as the best of friends, befitting the sisters they were, and Marti had become good friends with both Lizzie and Amelie too.

She had given Amelie the gift of life from her own bone marrow after all and, despite her mother's desire to keep it a secret from the world, this smart girl had done her own figuring out, her mother had only told her she needed to be tested to see if she matched, so of course she had gone directly to the man who was her true father, determined to know the truth.

Cathy talked with Marti about her own need to give forgiveness to William, she could withhold nothing from her, and Marti was pleased.

Marti told Cathy she loved her Mum, despite her awful behaviour over Martin, but she herself had always had a soft spot for her Uncle William, she liked him better than her own named father, truth be told. Now she at last understood why, she really was his daughter and preferred it this way.

She said she understood Cathy's dilemma, that there was no undoing that past awfulness but in the end his act of goodness had not only rescued Amelie, but rescued his own humanity. So, in this place, Cathy found a start of forgiveness in her soul for this man and his past.

Cathy knew she now needed to see William and thank him. She thought perhaps she would take a photo of Amelie at next Sunday's birthday party and bring it to him in jail, perhaps Amelie could also draw a little picture to go with it.

She had rung the jail at the start of the third week when Amelie seemed to have turned the corner and eaten her first solid food and she had rung again the day before they brought their daughter home and asked the warder to tell him the news with her thanks.

But it was not enough, she needed to go and see him in person and give him her own thanks, just her this next time, even though both Lizzie and Mathew had offered to come. But it was too personal and private to share, she wanted to see this new father again one more time with her own eyes, to try and look deeper and see what made him what he was without others intruding.

She had a sense that this was what she owed him, to try and reach understanding without judging what he had done in his life, not just on the one night when she had been conceived, but to try and get a value of his whole life

Robbie was her real father, the man who had loved her as his own child and raised her. Nothing would ever take that away and she knew he understood that.

But this man was a core part of her being, the other half of her genes, shared with her mother. So her biology required her to know who he was, perhaps to meet his own mother, her other unknown grandmother, or his sister. Even though as yet unknown to her they were an inextricable part of her family now.

So she had decided, as soon as the birthday party was over, and she had a photo developed of her daughter, she would take this and go and visit William, ask him to tell her about himself and his own family. He would never be a saint, perhaps not even a good man, but she, his daughter, needed to know him.

Then, perhaps when that was done, if Lizzie and Mathew and even Robbie and Gran wanted, they could come too and say their own thanks for his gift of life. Even though Marti had ended up donating the bone marrow cells, she did not think her daughter would have survived that first night without his blood and beyond that none of it would have happened without him.

Tomorrow she would ring the prison and make an arrangement for a visit at the end of next week.

That night she and Mathew shared the duties of saying good night and tucking Amelie into bed. As they were both giving last kisses and hugs and preparing to leave Amelie turned to her father with great solemnity and said. "Daddy, I need to talk to Mummy alone, I hope you don't mind, but I want you to come back in and give me one last kiss after I have finished."

It sounded so adult that he grinned and left, saying, "Of course my pet," as he closed the door behind him.

Amelie turned to look at her mother now with those same big solemn eyes. "Mummy, I want to go and visit my other Grandpa in jail, Grandpa William, the one who gave me the blood and found Marti who gave the bone marrow that let me get better.

"Sophie and I have both talked about it and we both agree I am well enough to go now and so I would like you to bring me to see him. Perhaps we could go tomorrow."

Catherine tried to suggest that they should wait a week, telling of her plans to take a picture at the birthday party and bring it in to him.

Amelie looked at her mother seriously and said, "That is OK, you can visit him then if you want, that is something for you to do. But I don't want to wait until then, and he does not need a photo if he sees me. Then he will have a picture inside his head of the real me. So please ring up in the morning and see if we can go and visit him tomorrow."

Catherine nodded, albeit reluctantly. "OK, I will ring tomorrow if that is what you want."

"Yes, thank you Mummy. Now you can go and tell Daddy to come back in, I will tell him what I am going to do and give him his last goodnight kiss."

Chapter 33 - Thank you from Amelie and Sophie

It took two days until the visit could be arranged at ten o'clock in the morning. Amelie said that was OK, she could wait until then.

That morning she chose her own dress, a pretty pale pink one with matching shoes. To bring with her Amelie carried a piece of paper folded over that she would not let Catherine or Mathew look at.

They caught a taxi to Malabar, slowly making their way through the mid-morning traffic. At the jail they were led down a corridor and then another corridor, it was a different building to where Catherine had been before. She realised it was no longer the high security part and was glad.

At the end of the second corridor they were brought to a door with a glass view pane and no bars in evidence. The warder opened the door and ushered them in, pointing to two seats at a table opposite a sitting man.

It took a second for Catherine to realise this man was William. The manacles were gone, he was neatly shaved and dressed and the deep anger which seemed to have scarred his previous demeanour was gone.

He looked up at them both and Catherine took a seat opposite and turned to lift Amelie up beside her.

But Amelie had instead walked to the other side of the table and was now holding out her arms, saying, "Lift me up Grandpa William."

He lifted her up to place her on his lap. Instead she hugged herself to his neck, drew back and planted a kiss on his cheek."

Then, earnestly, she opened the paper she was holding and spread it on the table before him. It was a picture of a big stick figure and two small stick figures, each holding a hand of the big person. There were some wavy lines underneath and some other wavy squiggles behind the people

"This is a picture of Sophie and me; she is the one with the hair," she said, pointing to some spiky things growing out of one small head. "I am the one with no hair," she said pointing to the other person. "We are on the beach, walking along with you, one day when you get out of prison. I am looking forward to that day. This picture is to say thank you from Sophie and me for saving my life."

The big man was silent, he just looked at the little girl with glistening eyes; then he gently stroked her cheek and put a big arm around her small shoulder. She lay her head against his cheek.

At last he spoke, "Thank you granddaughter, Thank you Amelie. Please say thank you to Sophie too."

Chapter 34 - Ten Years Later

It is a perfect summer's day at Little Bay; the beach under the rocky cliffs is lapped by wavelets. A picnic rug is spread on the sand, spread with picnic food. Five people sit in the sand, looking fondly into the water.

As one looks closer one recognises them; all a few years older. The two men are sharing a joke from a recent fishing trip; they have a similarity in body shape and features, though one looks about ten years older than the other.

The three women sit together, not talking but watching the beach with comfortable familiarity. It is clear they are all family, three generations, grandmother, mother and adult daughter.

In the water an older and powerfully built man plays with three children, one of whom sits on his shoulders. She looks to be about twelve though her figure is thin and waif like. She has funny spiky hair which pokes up from her head at odd angles, it won't submit to be flattened by the water. Her face is thin but striking with big wide eyes and an ethereal beauty. Tugging at the man's hands are a boy of about nine or ten and a girl a couple years younger, both bodies a picture of robust and healthy childhood.

The boy calls out, "Grandpa William, it is not fair, Amelie has been sitting on your shoulders for too long and now it's my turn."

About the Author

Graham Wilson lives in Sydney Australia. He has completed and published nine books, including three in this Old Balmain House Series.

His first novel in this series, tells the story of a small girl who went missing 100 years ago with her best friend and was never found, leaving a trail of grief down through generations until the finally her story is discovered. It is based in the real Balmain, an early inner Sydney suburb, with its real locations and historical events providing part of the story background. The second novel in this series, 'Lizzie's Tale' builds on "The Old Balmain House" setting, It is the story of a working class teenage girl who lives in this same house in the 1950s and 1960s, It tells of how she becomes pregnant she is determined not to surrender her baby for adoption, and her struggle to survive. The series concludes with this book 'Devils Choice' which follows the life of Lizzie's daughter Catherine and the awful choice she too must make through confronting her mother's rapists.

Graham has also written five novels in the Crocodile Dreaming Series. The first novel 'An English Visitor' tells the story of an English backpacker, Susan, who visits the Northern Territory and becomes captivated and in great danger from a man who loves crocodiles. The second book in the series, 'Crocodile Man', follows the consequences of the first book based around the discovery of this man's remains and the main character being placed on trial for murder. The third book, 'Girl in an Empty Cage', is about the struggle of the main character to retain her sanity in jail while her family and friends desperately try to find out what really happened on that fateful day before it is too late. Book 4, 'Lost Girl Diary' is the story of four missing backpackers whose lives are revealed in this man's diary. It is also the story of the search for the main character who has vanished too. Book 5, 'Dance with Shadows' concludes the series and begins with a girl who appears in a remote aboriginal community with no memory and how she rebuilds her life but alongside this come dark shadows that threaten to overwhelm her.

Graham has also written a family memoir "Children of Arnhem's Kaleidoscope." It tells of his childhood in an aboriginal community in remote Arnhem Land, in Australia's Northern Territory, one of its last frontiers. It tells of the people, danger and beauty of this place, and of its transformation over the last half century with the coming of aboriginal rights and the discovery or uranium. It also tells of his surviving an attack by a large crocodile.

In his non writing life he is a veterinarian who has worked with zoo animals, on large cattle stations and in national parks across many parts of Australia.

More information about Graham and his books and writing is available from the following sites:

Graham Wilson – Australian Author on Facebook
Graham Wilson Author Profile on Smashwords and Amazon

If you want to contact Graham directly please use the email:
grahambbbooks@gmail.com

www.ingramcontent.com/pod-product-compliance
Lightning Source LLC
Chambersburg PA
CBHW021017120726
47905CB00009B/3048